James Bayles

## Lowell

Past, present and prospective

James Bayles

**Lowell**
*Past, present and prospective*

ISBN/EAN: 9783337425845

Printed in Europe, USA, Canada, Australia, Japan

Cover: Foto ©Andreas Hilbeck / pixelio.de

More available books at **www.hansebooks.com**

# LOWELL:

# Past, Present and

# Prospective.

## 1891.

# INTRODUCTION.

This pamphlet was compiled and prepared with a view to presenting in a concise and available form, certain important facts regarding the city of Lowell — its industries, its enterprises and its prospects. Great pains were taken to collect the statistics which are as nearly accurate as an unofficial collation could possibly be.

The large four-page map, found elsewhere in the pamphlet, was especially prepared for this volume from the new maps of the U. S. survey, and it is of interest because it embraces a territory which very little exceeds the area of the city of Worcester. On this map will be found letters which refer to land elsewhere described which is available for manufacturing purposes.

There is much valuable information within the covers of this pamphlet, and an abundance of evidence to show that for investment, particularly in manufactures, there are few places more suitable and desirable than Lowell.

At the beginning of the present century, East Chelmsford was a hamlet with a tavern where the men and beasts that passed over the highways leading from Vermont and New Hampshire to Boston and Salem, found rest and refreshment.

The Merrimack and Concord rivers ran " unfettered to the sea," and the memory of the red man was still fresh in the minds of the hardy settlers who had wrested the land from his barbarous possession.

Eight years before, " the proprietors of the Locks and Canals on Merrimack River " had been incorporated, and had built the Pawtucket canal from above Pawtucket falls to the Concord river. Through this canal, the boats which came down the Merrimack passed to Newburyport and the sea, and the lumbermen no longer dreaded the turbulent waters of the rapids which had made their occupation so full of danger.

In twenty years the hamlet had become a village of two hundred and fifty inhabitants, and it boasted among other industrial advantages a cotton mill at Pawtucket falls, the Whipple powder mills, a flannel mill, several grist and saw mills, and a water highway to Boston harbor.

The Middlesex canal was projected in 1793 and was completed in 1804. Its original cost was $500,000; but its stockholders paid in assessments, $600,000 before they realized any dividend.

The canal ran from a point about a mile above Pawtucket falls, to Charlestown. The initial expense was so great that the stockholders received no benefit; but there is every reason to believe, that the canal would, in time, have become a source of profit.

Fisher & Ames built a dam at Massic falls on the Concord river, about 1820 and used the water to operate their forging mills. Moses Whipple had amassed a fortune in the manufacture of gunpowder and built the Whipple canal, which was afterwards extended and called the Wamesit canal.

But the creative hand of enterprise had not touched the mighty force of the noble Merrimack; nor had it even entered the minds of the simple villagers, that their fields and pastures were so soon to become the site of a great and throbbing city.

To Francis Cabot Lowell more than to any other man, is New England indebted for the cotton industries which form such an important factor in its commercial prestige. With Patrick T. Jackson he, in 1813, purchased a water power in Waltham, and secured an act of incorporation. In this enterprise they were joined by Nathan Appleton.

One of their first acts was to secure the services of Paul Moody, a clever mechanic of Amesbury.

Mr. Lowell, having obtained all possible information regarding the power loom then being introduced in England, built an improvement on that great invention which was adopted in the Waltham mills. Other improvements were made by Messrs. Lowell and Moody, and it was the latter who simplified the spinning process by spinning the filling directly on the cops without the process of winding.

While devoting his inventive skill to the perfecting of machinery, Mr. Lowell gave considerable thought to the improvement of those he employed. He had seen the degraded state of the operatives in England, and his chief endeavor, next after the fitting of his mill, was to ensure such domestic comforts and restrictions as would warrant the parents of New England in letting their daughters enter his employment. He provided boarding houses conducted by reputable women, furnished opportunities for religious worship, and established rules which were a safeguard against the evils which assail the young who are beyond parental supervision.

Mr. Lowell died in 1817, at the early age of 42.

The Waltham mill was a success. Mr. Appleton thought there was no reason why they should not manufacture and print calicoes in America. Mr. Jackson admitted that the operations were feasible; so the directors of the Waltham company began to look for a new water power. They went to the falls of the Souhegan, but did not find them satisfactory.

It was Ezra Worthen, of Salisbury, who suggested to Mr. Moody that they buy the Pawtucket canal, and acting upon his advice, Jackson and Appleton, with Kirk Boott, set about the purchase. They shrewdly secured the services of Thomas Clark, the agent of the canal company, through whom they were enabled to secure stock and land. They did not pay any more than they could help, and land that was bought at $200 an acre was sold by them at from 12 cents to $1 a foot, a year later.

In November, 1821, Jackson, Appleton, Kirk Boott, J. W. Boott, Moody and Warren Dutton visited the site of the future Lowell. They were mightily pleased with their bargain, as well they might have been; and somebody made the remark that it was quite possible they would live to see the place contain twenty thousand inhabitants.

The articles of association were drawn up on the 1st of December 1821. They described the association as the Merrimack Manufacturing Company with a capital stock of $600,000 divided into six hundred shares. The amount of assessments was limited to $1000, and Kirk Boott was engaged as treasurer and agent for five years at a salary of $3000 a year.

The company was incorporated Feb. 5, 1822, and the following directors were chosen: Warren Dutton, Patrick T. Jackson, Nathan Appleton, William Appleton, Israel Thorndike, Jr., John W. Boott; Kirk Boott, treasurer and clerk.

Everything was now in readiness for the new epoch. Kirk Boott was a man of decided and somewhat imperious manner. He had fought with Wellington on the Peninsula, although a native of Boston, and his military training, while it fitted him for the work he was selected to ac-

complish, made him exacting and arbitrary. But he enjoyed the full confidence of his associates, and the moment he was invested with authority, that moment he touched the lever which set in motion the progress which developed a great city.

The Merrimack Company paid $48,556 for the rights in the Pawtucket canal and for the land along its banks.

In the spring of 1822, work was begun. The canal was widened and deepened at a cost of $160,000; the foundation of the mills was laid; a house for Mr. Boott was built as also were the boarding houses.

The first wheel of the Merrimack Company was started on the 1st of September, 1823, and three additional mills were built. The first dividend of $100 a share was paid in 1825.

In 1824, St. Anne's church was built and Theodore Edson installed as pastor.

In 1825, five hundred dollars were appropriated for a library. The directors of the company never for a moment lost sight of the philanthropic design of Mr. Lowell, and the greatest care was taken to secure the comfort and happiness of the operatives. And they were very comfortable and very happy despite the fact that they labored fourteen hours a day.

In 1826 Mr. John D. Prince came from England and took charge of the calico printing, and it was his skill and executive ability that established the reputation and standing of the Merrimack prints, now so famous.

Thus did the Merrimack Company become the parent of all the industries that followed it. It is now in its 66th year, and what a family has been gathered about it! What activity, what energy, and what enterprise! "The speculation of the merchants of Boston," as Chevalier called it, has been a profitable one; it has benefitted not only the inventors but the thousands who have come to operate its machinery and conduct its rapidly increasing business. Prosperity and peace have been its privileges, and they have come with a quiet modesty which constrasts very strongly with the blare and rumpus of the booming so characteristic of some breezy sections. They were conservative men who worked such radical changes in the industrial character of New England and of Lowell, and while the progress is still directed with a liberal resolve, the guiding principle is a conservative one.

In October, 1824, the Merrimack Company increased its capital to $1,200,000 and sold all its rights in the Pawtucket canal, together with the land, to the Proprietors of the Locks and Canals, who were authorized to purchase, hold, lease or sell land and water power to the amount of $600,000. Mr. Boott was the first agent of the canal company. He was succeeded by Joseph Tilden and Patrick T. Jackson, and in 1845 James B. Francis was appointed to that position.

Mr. Francis came to this country from England when a lad of 18. He was the son of a civil engineer and was so fortunate as to find employment upon his arrival in America under George Whistler, the eminent engineer. When Whistler came to Lowell to take charge of the Machine shop, Mr. Francis came with him and was, in 1837, appointed chief engineer for the canal company. In 1846 he projected and built the Northern canal, a monument to hydraulic ingenuity and skill as imperishable as the reputation of him who built it. He also designed the guard locks which stand an impregnable barrier between the city and the flood.

When we have said that the enterprise of Appleton, Boott and Jackson was followed by the speedy incorporation of the Hamilton, the Appleton, the Lowell, the Middlesex, the Suffolk, the Tremont, the Lawrence, the Bleachery, the Boott and the Massachusetts companies in their order, we have said all that need be said in justification of the wisdom that prompted the selection of the hamlet of East Chelmsford as the place of an industry which has enriched so many and kept so many more in the comforts of plenty.

## LOWELL IN 1870.

### THE LOWELL OF 20 YEARS AGO AND THE PROMISE IT GAVE OF THE FUTURE.

Until 1836 Lowell was still a town, but that year it acquired the right and title to municipal privileges. Its progress had been phenomenal. In ten years it developed beyond the expectations of its founders. Its mills were running at a profit, and its goods had acquired a reputation which made the demand greater than the capacity for production.

The companies increased their works and the best and the steadiest of New England's men and women came here to earn a livelihood. It was these pioneers of the cotton industry that established the standard of intelligent labor in Lowell that not even the fell tide of immigration has been able to overthrow. There is nowhere in the United States a class of labor so intelligent and so reliable as that which toils in Lowell.

All went swimmingly until the panic of 1857. The cotton mills of Lowell suffered with the other industries of the country. The companies had scarcely recovered from the effects of the panic when the war broke out. With a singular lack of foresight, many of the companies discharged their help and sold their cotton. When peace was declared business was resumed and has been continued with remarkable steadiness ever since.

For purpose of comparison we will endeavor briefly to show what Lowell was in 1870.

It had a population of 40,928. Its area was 3838 acres and it had 50 miles of streets. It had 5421 houses and its total valuation was $25,922,488. It had 4¾₁₀₀ of street railway tracks and its polls were 8577.

There were but fifteen manufacturing corporations in Lowell in 1870. These were the Machine shop, Wamesit steam mill, Appleton, Boott, Hamilton, Lawrence, Lowell, Massachusetts, Merrimack, Middlesex, Suffolk, Tremont, Belvidere Woolen mills, Bleachery and the Lowell Hosiery. To these may be added the Wamesit Power company, the Proprietors of the Locks and Canals, the Lowell Gas Light company, the Boston & Lowell, Lowell & Nashua and Lowell & Lawrence railroads, twenty-two in all. The total valuation of these corporations was $12,262,319.

There were published at that time two daily papers, the *Courier* and the *Citizen*, and the *Vox Populi* was issued semi-weekly.

## LOWELL IN 1891.

### THE LOWELL OF TO-DAY, — ITS AREA, VALUATION AND POPULATION.

The Lowell of 1891, with a population of 80,000, stands 37 in the list of important cities in the United States, and its right to be known as the "Manchester of America" there is none to dispute. Its area has been five times increased by annexation, and it still remains the most condensed municipal community in New England. In 1834, that quarter known as Belvidere was annexed from Tewksbury; in 1851 Centralville was annexed from Dracut; in 1874 Middlesex Village and a portion of Dracut were annexed. In 1879, 395 acres were annexed from Dracut, and in 1888 192 acres were annexed from Tewksbury. The annexation of 1879 was largely one of sentiment. It was found after the annexation of 1874 that four families living in Dracut, quite near the Tyngsboro line, were deprived of school advantages, and that the children might receive an education, the city annexed the additional territory.

The total area of Lowell is now 7932 acres or 12 11/50 square miles. Its congested character is shown in the following table based upon the census of 1885:

| | POPULATION. | | ACRES. |
|---|---|---|---|
| Worcester | 68,389 | | 22,900 |
| Springfield | 37,575 | | 20,817 |
| Haverhill | 21,795 | | 15,200 |
| Gloucester | 21,703 | | 14,000 |
| Fall River | 56,870 | | 17,749 |
| Taunton | 23,674 | | 33,200 |
| Holyoke | 27,895 | | 10,038 |
| New Bedford | 33,393 | | 11,113 |

In 1890, Lowell had 11,200 dwellings and its valuation was $62,046,799, an increase of $36,074,311 over that of 1870 Its polls were 19,833, and the length of its accepted streets, 104 miles, 8 4/5 miles of which are paved with granite. It has of well built sewers, 55 6/10 miles. Its water works are the finest in New England, and its gas is the cheapest furnished by any city in the East.

It has now forty incorporated companies engaged in manufactures of various kinds and its railroad facilities are of an exceptionally convenient character. The Lowell and Suburban Street Railway Company has over 27 miles of track and the company contemplates many changes in the immediate future that will greatly benefit the community.

The total valuation of the incorporated companies is $26,224,115.

There are employed in the mills and workshops 31,120 persons, divided as follows:

| | | |
|---|---|---|
| Textile | | 24,172 |
| Machinery | | 2,838 |
| Wool | | 1,050 |
| Leather | | 560 |
| Cartridges, Paper, Etc., Etc. | | 2,500 |
| | | 31,120 |

Fully 20,000 persons are employed in professions, domestic duties, trade and business other than manufacturing. And it will be readily admitted that Lowell has an industrious population. Almost 53 per cent. of the entire population is in active employment.

The character of the population is made manifest in a most creditable manner in the statistics we give elsewhere of the the savings banks, and to say nothing of the churches and theatres which exercise a moral influence on the community. Here we have neither riots nor strikes. There is little or no vagabond element, nor is there any of those socialistic agitations which so frequently disturb the prosperity of manufacturing communities. The 11,200 dwellings show that a large proportion of the wage earners are housed in their own homes, and in no other manufacturing community is the number of homes thus owned so great.

The city enjoys an exceptional system of water works, introduced and perfected at a cost of over $4,000,000. Its police and fire departments are adequate; its schools numerous and well provided; it has an efficient board of health, and a free public library of 45,000 volumes. There was appropriated for the current municipal expenses of the year 1891, $918,200.

The clearing house returns show business transactions, aside from those of the large corporations, amounting to $40,000,000 in the year 1890.

The number of industries has been greatly increased and diversified within

# 11

the past ten years, and fortunes have been made in the transfers of real estate.

There are now in course of construction a federal building for the accommodation of the post office, at a cost of $250,000, a city hall and memorial building, the latter to be used for library purposes, at a joint cost of $500,000.

The city maintains the Rogers' Fort Hill park, elevated 200 feet above the level of the city, two spacious commons and two small parks. It has just completed a magnificent boulevard, two miles long, on the northerly bank of the Merrimack river.

That the spirit of enterprise is rife among our men of business may be seen in what is published elsewhere in this pamphlet regarding street railways, the erection of buildings and the offers that are made of sites for new industries. This spirit is stimulated by the Board of Trade and the Master Builders' exchange, and by various syndicates and individuals.

## PUBLIC BUILDINGS.

STRUCTURES WHICH COMMEND THE ENTERPRISE AS THEY INDICATE THE FINANCIAL AND INDUSTRIAL STANDING OF THE CITY.

The present city hall was built to convenience the officers of the town. It is an unpretentious structure which has afforded doubtful accommodation to the officers of the city these many years. Its successor will be a magnificent structure of Conway granite, three stories with a spacious basement, and decorated with a tower 180 feet high. The building will contain handsome chambers for the city council and school board, and offices for the heads of all departments. It was designed by Merrill & Cutler and will cost when completed $350,000.

The city library is at present confined to narrow and hampered quarters in the Masonic building. Here it quite recently suffered serious damage by fire. When there was talk of erecting a monument to Lowell's dead soldiers, public meetings were held to decide what form the monument should have.

The consensus of opinion favored a Memorial building which should be utilized in part for library purposes. The city council generously made an appropriation of $150,000 for such a structure and the plans of F. W. Stickney were accepted. These provide for an ornate building in every way worthy its high memorial character. It will be built of Conway granite and will have a central tower. Here the library will have ample and fireproof accommodations.

Both these buildings will be located on a large triangular lot at the junction of Merrimack and Moody streets. Work begun on them last Fall and the first stories of each are nearing completion.

Through the efforts of Hon. Charles H. Allen, then representing the Seventh district, Congress in 1889 made an appropriation of $200,000 for a federal building to be erected in Lowell. The government was given the site at the corner of Appleton and Gorham streets formerly occupied by St. Peter's church. Plans have been prepared and the contracts awarded, and work will begin at an early date under the experienced direction of Colonel James W. Bennett who has been appointed supervisor of construction. The building will be classical in design and will be a decided ornament to the city.

When the military companies were deprived by fire of their armory in Middle street, the state commissioners secured a lot of land on Westford street and erected thereon the present imposing structure. It has a castellated facade and is a model of military convenience. Its commanding position makes it a landmark for many sections of the city. It was built at a cost of $90,000.

The High school building was erected in 1840. Like the city hall, it has shrunk far behind the necessities of the age. It is in a very crowded condition. The city council has obtained authority to borrow $150,000 for a new building and plans prepared by F. W. Stickney have been accepted. The new building will stand upon the site of the old one, which will be enlarged by the purchase of two adjoining lots. It will be in every respect a model institution, and architecturally it will be a credit both to its designer and the city.

The city owns many handsome school buildings and provisions have been made for the erection of a new Moody school building in Belvidere.

The central fire station in Palmer street is an unusually fine building, and the stations in various parts of the city are substantially built of brick and stone.

The county jail on Thorndike street is a large double-towered building of gray granite, conspicuous for its architectural grace as it is for its evident strength.

The buildings at the city farm are plain and substantial and are of quite recent construction.

## PRIVATE BUILDINGS.

### WHERE BUSINESS IS TRANSACTED AND PEOPLE DWELL.

Within the last fifteen years, there have been many changes for the better in the character and design of our business blocks. The Masonic temple, built by the late Hocum Hosford, was the pioneer of private enterprise in that direction. The Five Cent savings bank is established in an elegant marble building. The Hildreth Building, in which the post office is located, and the Central Block, built by the Tyler heirs, are perhaps the two most completely equipped and largest business blocks in the city. The Runels Block, now in course of construction at the corner of Bridge and Merrimack streets, and the Howe Block in the opposite corner, will rival these, both in their architectural features and interior arrangements.

The Odd Fellows Building now being built will be modern in design and development. The Hoyt and Shedd Building, the Appleton Bank Building, the First National Bank Building, the Old Lowell Bank Building, the Mansur Block, the Ingham Block, the Stott Block, the St. Charles Hotel, the Merrimack House, the American House, the Richardson Block, the St. Cloud Hotel, the Glidden Block, the Swan Building, the Spalding Building, the Fiske Building, the Cook & Taylor Block, the Hosford Building, Wyman's Exchange are only a few of the many costly buildings devoted to business.

There are some notable residences in Lowell. That of Gen. Butler's in Belvidere is a substantial house such as was built by country gentlemen 50 years ago.

The Nesmith mansion, the Fellows house and the Hovey house are buildings of similar character. On the hill are the stone residences of Hon. A. P. Bonney and Frederick Faulkner. The residences of Hon. F. W. Howe, Thomas Carolin, A. G. Pollard, A. G. Cumnock, T. G. Tweed, Dr. H. P. Jefferson, F. P. Putnam, Hon. Charles A. Stott, Mrs. Wm. A. Burke, W. S. Lamson, W. H. Anderson, and F. B. Shedd, are types in the Belvidere district. In the Highlands, there is the mansion of Hon. W. E. Livingston, and a host of more modern dwellings of which those of Mayor Fifield, W. A. Ingham, Hon. John J. Donovan, David Horne, C. W. Wilder, Col. J. W. Bennett, Mrs. Sidney Spalding and C. J. Glidden are characteristic specimens.

In Ward Five, there are many fine residences. Among them those of Mrs. James Minter, Frederick Ayer, Hon. C. H. Allen, Mrs. Robert H. Butcher, Jacob Rogers, Sewall G. Mack, Lucy Fay, Mrs. J. C. Ayer, H. M. Thompson, A. A. Coburn, H. C. Perham and Thos. Stott.

In Centralville there are the Parker, the Read and the Hildreth mansions, the Barker residence and the residences of Major E. T. Rowell, John H. McAlvin, Harry R. Raynes and Mrs. A. H. Boardman.

In every district and on every hand the houses, if not distinctive of great wealth, are eloquent of comfort and good taste.

## WATERWAYS AND CANALS.

### LOWELL'S RIVERS, BROOKS AND CANALS AND NUMEROUS BRIDGES.

Lowell is bountifully supplied with water. The Merrimack river which rises in the White mountains also drains Lake Winnipesaukee, a body of water covering seventy square miles. This majestic stream flows in a sinuous course of nearly six miles through the city, and affords a force equivalent to 10,000 horse power. Its average width is 600 feet.

The Concord river flows two and a quarter miles within the city boundaries, and joins the Merrimack at a point one mile and a fraction from the Dracut boundary line. Its average width is 200 feet, and it supplies 500 horse power.

River Meadow Brook is two and a quarter miles long and flows into the Concord river. It serves numerous industries with a 50 horse power.

Stony Brook flows through Forge Village, Graniteville and Chelmsford into the Merrimack a quarter of a mile above the city line. It furnishes 50 horse power.

Beaver Brook rises in Windham, and furnishes power for two mills in Dracut before it empties into the Merrimack at the city boundaries.

The system of canals by which the waters of the Merrimack are conveyed to the mills is over five miles in length.

The following table shows the exact length of the waterways within the city limits:

|  | FEET. |
|---|---|
| Merrimack River | 31,250 |
| Concord " | 12,750 |
| River Meadow Brook | 12,000 |
| Beaver Brook | 2,000 |
| Northern Canal | 4,373 |
| Western " | 4,472 |
| Tremont " | 575 |
| Moody Street Feeder | 1,375 |
| Pawtucket Canal | 9,188 |
| Merrimack " | 2,586 |
| Hamilton " | 1,770 |
| Eastern " | 1,913 |
| Boott Penstock | 235 |
|  | 85,087 |

Total length 16 miles 607 feet.

There are three other brooks of variant character which are not included in the above list.

The canals and rivers divide the city into seven islands, six of which are thickly populated.

The Pawtucket canal was originally built in 1796 for the purpose of making the river navigable for boats, rafts and masts. In 1822 Nathan Appleton, Patrick T. Jackson, Kirk Boott and others bought the Pawtucket canal and directed its waters to manufacturing purposes. They built the Pawtucket dam, widened the canal to 60 feet and built the Merrimack canal. In 1825 The Proprietors of the Locks and Canals were incorporated and secured by charter all rights in the waters of the Merrimack for manufacturing purposes. Mr. James B. Francis, after eleven years of service as engineer, was appointed agent in 1845, and remained at the head of the company's affairs until 1885, when he accepted the honor of consulting engineer and retired. He was succeeded by his son, Col. James Francis.

The Merrimack canal was completed in 1823; the Western canal in 1831, and the Eastern canal in 1835. They were originally fed by the Pawtucket canal. The first supplies power to the Machine shop, Lowell, Merrimack and Sherman's grist mills; the second supplies power to the Tremont, Lawrence and Merrimack mills, and the last supplies the Prescott, Massachusetts and Boott mills.

The Northern canal was built in 1847–48 under the direction of Mr. James B. Francis. The massive parapet of masonry which extends along the south shore of the river, holds the waters of the canal 50 feet above the river bed, and is a triumph of engineering skill. It is connected with the Western, Merrimack and Eastern canals.

The Wamesit canal was built in 1846, and carries the waters of the Concord to a number of mills. It supplies 500 horse power.

Where there is so much water in natural and artificial channels, there must of necessity be many bridges. There are 209 bridges in Lowell, 100 of which are on public thoroughfares.

The bridges crossing the Merrimack are substantial structures. The present Pawtucket bridge was built in 1871; the Aiken street bridge in 1883; and the present Central bridge in the same year. All three are iron bridges.

## POPULATION.

According to the census of 1890, Lowell had a population of 77,696.

This is an increase of 13,589 over the census of 1885, the figures of which were 64,107.

Here is an increase of 21 per cent. in five years.

A year has elapsed since the census of 1890 was taken. Admitted that the per centage of the preceding five years was maintained in the year which has elapsed since the last census was taken, and we should have an additional increase of a fraction over 4 per cent., or 3200.

This, added to 77,696, would make a population of 80,896. It is no exaggeration to say the figures exceed 81,000 at this time.

Lowell has an area of only 7932 acres.

Worcester has an area of 22,809 acres and a population by the last census of 84,655.

If Lowell covered as much territory as Worcester does it would embrace the villages of North and West Chelmsford, Chelmsford Centre, North Billerica, the most populous section of Dracut and portions of Tyngsboro and Tewksbury.

With an area of 22,000 acres Lowell would have a population of 86,000.

The business of the city represents in actual figures not less than 90,000 people. It, is the market place of Billerica, Carlisle, Chelmsford, Westford, Dunstable, Tyngsboro, Littleton, Acton, a portion of Pelham, N. H., Dracut, Tewksbury and a large section of Andover.

According to the census of 1880, 52 per cent. of the entire population was in active employment. The statistics showing the industry of the people are not yet tabulated for the returns of 1890, but it is safe to assume that the commendable percentage will not be lessened.

It is interesting to see in what degree the people were employed under the census of 1885.

There were at that time 28,517 males in Lowell and 35,590 females. The following were the occupations:

| | | | | | |
|---|---|---|---|---|---|
| Government | · | · | · | · | 299 |
| Professions | · | · | · | · | 911 |
| Domestic | · | · | · | · | 14,920 |
| Personal service | · | · | · | 840 |
| Trade | · | · | · | · | 2941 |
| Transportation | · | · | · | 1100 |

| | | | | |
|---|---|---|---|---|
| Agriculture | · | · | · | 458 |
| Laborers | · | · | · | 1290 |
| Apprentices | · | · | · | 135 |
| Children at work | · | · | 250 |
| Manufacturing | · | · | 21,454 |
| | | | | 44,598 |

To these may be added :

| | | | | | |
|---|---|---|---|---|---|
| Scholars | · | · | · | · | 9568 |
| Students | · | · | · | · | 183 |
| Retired | · | · | · | · | 715 |
| Non-productive | · | · | · | 593 |
| Dependents | · | · | · | 263 |
| At home | · | · | · | · | 7424 |
| Not given | · | · | · | · | 703 |
| | | | | | 19,449 |

And here is a significant item. In a population of 64,000 there were only returned as out of employment for 12 months, 40 people.

It may not be without interest to know the nativity of the population of Lowell. According to the census of 1885 the proportions are as follows :

| BORN IN : | | | | |
|---|---|---|---|---|
| Massachusetts | · | · | · | 25,631 |
| Other states in New England | · | 10,372 |
| Other states | · | · | · | 2221 |
| Ireland | · | · | · | 11,681 |
| Canada (French) | · | · | · | 6438 |
| " (English) | · | · | · | 1380 |
| England | · | · | · | 3512 |
| Scotland | · | · | · | 785 |
| Nova Scotia | · | · | · | 621 |
| Prince Edward's Island | · | · | 135 |
| New Brunswick | · | · | · | 516 |
| Germany | · | · | · | 70 |
| Sweden | · | · | · | 275 |
| Portugal | · | · | · | 43 |
| Other countries | · | · | · | 427 |

Since 1885 the number of French-Canadians and of Swedes has largely increased. They form a thrifty, industrious and peaceable portion of the community.

From recent statistics we find the following conditional division of labor existing at the present time :

| | | | | |
|---|---|---|---|---|
| Manufacturers | · | · | · | 24,172 |
| Machinists | · | · | · | 2838 |
| Wood | · | · | · | 1050 |
| Leather | · | · | · | 560 |
| Cartridges, etc., etc. | · | · | 2500 |
| Professions | · | · | · | 1200 |
| Trade | · | · | · | 3760 |
| Domestic | · | · | · | 16,500 |
| Government | · | · | · | 432 |
| Transportation | · | · | · | 2340 |
| Agriculture | · | · | · | 480 |
| Laborers | · | · | · | 1600 |
| | | | | 57,432 |

# LABOR.

### THE PREEMINENTLY INTELLIGENT AND RELIABLE QUALITY ASSURED IN LOWELL.

When the Merrimack mills were first established, the operatives were drawn from the towns and villages of New England. They were sober, industrious and reliable people. The building of the mills attracted the immigrant labor. It was also of a sober and reliable quality, for fares were high in those days and it was only those who were seeking homes that came to the new town of Lowell. This foreign labor mingled with the native element and imbibed the best of its many admirable qualities.

As the industries developed, there was a demand for men skilled in the art of calico printing, and a superior class of workmen accordingly came from England and from other countries to add their intelligent influence to the moral progress of the community.

The corporations were under necessity to provide food and shelter for those they employed. They adopted Mr. Lowell's plan, so effectively instituted at Waltham, and built boarding and tenement houses. Over these a rigid supervision was maintained. The food in the former was required to be of a certain standard. The rules governing the conduct of those who lived in the boarding and tenement houses were rather strict; but they were wholesome; and although they have long since lapsed, their effect is still seen when the bells ring the curfew at nine o'clock every night.

There is still much of the native element employed in the mills, and the children of the immigrants who came here in the early days form an exceptionally intelligent portion of the community.

There are many French Canadians employed in the mills. They are very desirable operatives; they are steady, sober and industrious. They are thrifty and are more permanent than they used

to be. Many of them now own their homes, and their children fill positions where education is a prerequisite to success.

There have never been any serious strikes in Lowell. The only labor troubles it has ever experienced have arisen from isolated and petty differences which have been amicably settled without serious loss to employer or employee. Our corporations have always shown a liberal disposition to treat with their employes, and labor agitators of the blatant style have ever found Lowell to be a poor place for their disturbing purposes.

The foreign elements are chiefly represented by the French Canadians, the British, the Irish and the Swedes. Their chief ambition seems to be to own their homes, and the outlying districts are thickly settled with the people of their class. They can buy comfortable homes for from $1000 to $1500, and when they are so established they are not disposed to find fault with the means by which they enjoy such independence.'

The savings banks contain their earnings, and the fact that many of the influential men in the community were themselves at one time operatives in the mills, has an encouraging effect upon those who are now employed in their places.

There are no socialistic clubs or organizations in Lowell. Labor unions there are, of sparse membership, but they do not seem to be in favor with the operative class.

There is nowhere in the United States a more thrifty, intelligent and desirable class of help than can be found in Lowell, and the attendance at the free evening schools is a commendable evidence of the ambition which animates the young who are compelled by force of circumstances to earn their livelihood in our mills.

## COST OF LIVING.

### THE BENEFITS THE LOWELL SYSTEM CONFERS UPON THE ENTIRE COMMUNITY.

The cost of living in Lowell is lower than it is in any other city of its size and character in the United States. This is due to what is known as "the Lowell

system." When Francis C. Lowell established the cotton mills at Waltham, he made the shelter and food of the employes his especial care. He built substantial brick tenement and boarding houses and fixed the rentals and the price of board at low and stable figures.

When Jackson and Boott built the Merrimack mills they adopted the Lowell system. So, too, did the other corporations that followed. That system is still preserved, and when it is abandoned Lowell will lose one of its most distinctive features and one which gives it an advantage not enjoyed by other manufacturing communities.

There are no corporation stores, but the companies pay the boarding house keepers a small sum for every boarder. They let the boarding houses at extremely low figures and enforce a rule of conduct which, if not severe, is nevertheless wholesome.

Of the corporations, nine own tenement property valued at from $50,000 to $300,000 each. The average rent for a tenement of eight rooms is $7 a month; nine rooms rent for $8. These figures are the standard.

Tenements of four, five or six rooms can be procured anywhere in the city for from $6 to $8 a month; and very superior tenements, in the most desirable sections, are rented for $10 and $12 a month. There are tenements cheaper than those owned by the corporations, but they are very few and undesirable and their number is growing less.

It costs a man $2.90 to board a week in a corporation boarding house; a woman can board for $2.25. The food is substantial and of excellent quality. Outside, the price of board in many places is $3.00 for men and $2.50 for women. These figures include food and lodging. A weaver earning $10 a week can live for $117 a year and live well. It is little wonder then, that our savings banks contain more money than there is represented in the united capital of the great corporations.

We have here, in Lowell, a large market for the surrounding country. Vegetables are cheap, and the absence of high rents enable our dealers to offer their merchandise at prices all the way from 25 to 2 per cent. less than the prices charged in Boston and elsewhere.

A man earning $12 a week, and paying $156 for his board and lodgings for a year, can be well supplied with clothing, boots and underwear for $50. He can live in Lowell, be well dressed and comfortable, for $200 a year. If he is frugal he can save $300 a year, and many men do.

But the corporations aside, we have cheaper rents and cheaper board than can be obtained in any other city in Massachusetts. The wages may not quite touch the figures they do in other places; but the difference is more than compensated for in the reduced cost of living.

It has been predicted that some time in the future the corporations will be obliged to abandon their boarding houses and convert the property to manufacturing purposes. But there is nothing to warrant such a prediction.

An agent of one of our mills desiring to extend his works concluded to build upon the site of his tenements. But when he had reckoned the consequences he changed his plan and the tenements remained. The abandonment of the Lowell system means an increase in the price of board, and that, quite naturally, would excite a demand for larger wages. With that demand would come the opportunity the labor agitators have so long been looking for in this conservatively progressive and peaceful community.

## VOLUME OF BUSINESS.

### THE AGGREGATE OF MONEY REPRESENTED IN A YEAR'S MANUFACTURING.
### ($76,503,782.)

The industries of Lowell are manifold. The manufacture of cotton cloth was the first established and it is still the staple of our great trade. There are seven large corporations engaged in that industry, producing 257,800,000 yards of cloth per annum, and giving employment to 15,000 people.

There are 103,000,000 yards of calico dyed and printed every year.

The sales of these seven corporations for the year 1890 amounted to $19,572,556,

NEW CITY HALL.

and the total sum involved in their business was $34,889,861.

There are eight mills engaged in the manufacture of woollens and carpets. The volume of business transacted by them in 1890 aggregated $11,422,921.

There are twelve mills which manufacture elastic webbing, suspenders, hosiery, underwear, cotton and worsted yarn. Their business for 1890 aggregated $5,550,000.

There is besides the bleachery one other manufacturing dye works, and the aggregate of business done in that line was $1,000,500.

There are 26 machine shops in Lowell, the largest of which is the Lowell Machine Shop, with a capital of $900,000, employing 1500 men. Then comes the Kitson Machine Company, builders of cotton machinery. There are four foundries, exclusive of that in the Lowell Machine Shop. There are in addition to the American Bolt Company, several establishments for the manufacture of bolts and screws. Of other iron industries there are one manufacturer of scales, one of turbine water wheels, four wire workers, and two boiler makers. The aggregate of business done by all grades of iron workers during he year 1890, was $6,460,000.

There are six large lumber dealers in Lowell, four manufacturers of boxes, five of doors, sashes and blinds, one of coffins, one of bungs, one of clamps and screws, seven of furniture, two of refrigerators, two of stairs, one of tanks and vats and one of croquet sets. The aggregate of business done by these workers in wood for the year 1890, was $4,180,500.

There are no less than 26 manufacturers of mill supplies, doing a business aggregating $2,000,000 per annum.

Of miscellaneous industries such as cash carriers, shoes, etc., the aggregate will not fall short of $5,000,000. Nor does this include the money turned over in our patent medicine factories. The aggregate of business done in proprietary medicines and perfumes was over $6,000,000.

These figures are based upon actual returns.

| VOLUME OF MANUFACTURING BUSINESS, 1890. | |
|---|---|
| Cotton - - - - | $34,889,861 |
| Woollens and Carpets - | 11,422,921 |
| Hosiery, Yarn, Webbing - | 5,550,000 |
| Bleaching and dying - - | 1,000,500 |
| Machinery - - - | 6,460,000 |
| Wood working - - - | 4,180,500 |
| Mill supplies - - - | 2,000,000 |
| Medicines and perfumes - | 6,000,000 |
| Miscellaneous - - - | 5,000,000 |
| | 876,503,782 |

## FORTY MILLIONS

### TOTAL CLEARINGS, AND FORTY PER CENT. INCREASE IN FOUR YEARS.

Year by year the banks are becoming in a constantly increasing degree the accountants of the business transactions of their respective communities, and the work of the clearing houses summarizes the financial operations of the several cities wherein those institutions flourish. In this respect, however, Lowell is uniquely situated, inasmuch as the larger money dealings of her great manufacturing corporations are prosecuted by their treasurers in Boston, with the effect that the reports of the Lowell clearing house relate solely to the more strictly commercial exchanges resulting in the course of the local retail trade. Nevertheless, Lowell retains her position well in the face of this fact and of the fact that she does not profit by the adventitious aid of speculation, which so largely augments the clearings of more metropolitan cities, nor by the frequent and sometimes fictitious transfers of real estate which swell the totals of certain western places far beyond the actual interchange of cash.

The volume of business pursues a steady, healthy growth, and shows no signs of retreating upon the path it has followed during the past few years.

The clearing system began in Lowell March 22, 1876, as an experiment, and after less than a month's trial, on April 20, 1876, the Clearing House Association was organized under the following officers: Chairman, J. F. Kimball; vice chairman, G. B. Allen; secretary, A. A. Coburn; clearing house committee, C. M. Williams, G. W. Knowlton, C. W. Eaton; manager, J. S. Hovey. The clearing bank was first the Railroad National, and since then that duty has been performed in rotation. The present officers are C. M. Williams, chairman; G. W. Knowlton, vice chairman; F. Blanchard, secretary: E. K. Perley, W. M. Sawyer, F. P. Haggett, clearing house committee; W. W. Johnson, manager; and the Merchants National is the clearing bank. Amended articles of association were adopted July 15, 1889.

A fair comparison will show the rapidity of the recent growth of Lowell as can nothing else save the census returns.

Four years ago, from May 1, 1886, to May 1, 1887, the aggregate exchanges were $28,110,065.68, and the balances $8,862,952.84. In the year just concluded from May 1, 1890, to May 1, 1891, the clearings were $38.922,859.03, with balances of $11,560,908.16. Nearly forty millions of gross exchanges within a year marked by unprecedented financial depression all over the world, and despite adverse conditions, a showing of almost forty per cent. increase over the figures of four years since!

## BANKS OF DISCOUNT.

CAPITAL OF $2,225,000; DEPOSITS OF $4,300,288.45; SURPLUS OF $1,051,356.85.

Of the national banks and trust companies of Lowell it would be invidious to speak in terms of comparison. All are conservatively managed, paying liberal dividends to stockholders and giving plentiful accommodation to customers. The aggregate banking capital, the sum of the figures given in the heading to this article, appeared to be, at the time of the latest return to the comptroller of the currency, just $7,576,645.30, — exclusive of circulation, $543,650, and certificates of deposit, $271,170.51, which being added would produce a sum total of $8,391,465.81 : besides which must also be reckoned the aggregate assets of the savings banks, more than twice as much in addition.

The Appleton Bank was incorporated in 1847, and located in its own building at the corner of Central and Hurd streets, occupying the site of its present elegant block, which was erected in 1878. This bank has a capital of $300,000, surplus $130,000, undivided profits of $44,038 67, and deposits of almost exactly one million dollars. The dividends paid have averaged ten per cent. The officers are John F. Kimball, president; W. S. Bennett, H. H. Wilder, A. Putnam, W. E. Livingston, F. B. Shedd, F. A. Buttrick, J W. C. Pickering, G. W. Fifield, H. M. Knowles, G. O. Whiting, directors; E. K. Perley, cashier.

The First National Bank was organized under the national banking laws in 1864, with a capital of $250,000. In 1884 it removed from the old building at the corner of Central and Middle streets to its own handsome block, 40 Central street.

It has a surplus fund of $150,000, undivided profits of $30,067.19, and deposits of $549,329,96. J. C Abbott is president; E. Brown, S. N. Wood, G. Kimball, P. Dempsey, J. S. Brown, S. C. Taylor, W. H. Parker, J. Lennon, T. Costello, H. G. Cushing, directors; W. M. Sawyer, cashier.

The Prescott Bank was incorporated in 1850, being then located at the corner of Central and Market streets, whence it removed in 1865 to occupy its own block at 28 Central street, where it now is. It has a capital of $300,000, surplus of $100,000, undivided profits of $86,119.56, and deposits at the close of business May 4, 1891, of $134,598.84. Hapgood Wright is president; A. A. Coburn, vice-president; G. F. Richardson, C. H. Coburn, D. Gage, C. A. Stott. W. A. Ingham, J. W. Abbott, J. A. Bartlett, directors; F. Blanchard, cashier.

The Lowell Bank organized in 1828 became in 1865 the Old Lowell National Bank, and under these titles has occupied quarters consecutively as follows: Corner Merrimack and Worthen streets, the old Wyman's Exchange, Shattuck street, the new Wyman's Exchange; and it has just removed to its sumptuous apartments in the Bowditch building on Central street. Its capital is $200,000, surplus $40,000, undivided profits $27,758.79, and its deposits $309,467.96. John Davis is president; E. M. Tucke, P. Whiting, P. Parker, A. B. Woodworth, G. F. Penniman, W. W. Carey, J. L. Chalifoux, P. H. Donohoe, directors; C. M. Williams, cashier.

The Wamesit Bank, which occupies its own building at the corner of Middlesex and Thorndike streets, was incorporated in 1853, with a capital of $250,000. It has a surplus fund of $50,000, undivided profits of $41,803.58, and individual deposits of $323,815.71. H. C. Howe is the president; S. Horn, P. C. Gates, L. B. Hall, W. H. Wiggin, P. P. Perham, S. Kidder, F. Jewett, J. W. Bennett, directors; G. W. Knowlton, cashier.

The Merchants Bank occupies the ground floor of its own building, 39 Merrimack street, next west of Postoffice block. Its capital is $400,000, surplus $100,000, undivided profits $117,459.51, and it had deposits of $1,023,706.71 at the time of its last return. The president is A. P. Bonney; directors, W. H. Anderson, C. H. Latham, A. Pratt, W. Shepard, A. F. Nichols, Geo. Runels, F. T. Jaques, M. Collins, A. G. Pollard; cashier, W. W. Johnson. It was incorporated in 1854 and nationalized in 1864.

The Railroad Bank was organized in 1831, chiefly by Boston gentlemen and stockholders in our great manufacturing corporations. For forty years this bank did the business of the Lowell mills almost exclusively. It was first located at the corner of Central and Hurd streets, then in succession at the corner of Merrimack and John streets, on Shattuck street, in the Carleton block, and recently settled in its own building, 93, 95 and 97 Merrimack street. Its capital was once $800,000; but in 1885 was reduced to $400,000, just double what it began business with 54 years before. There is a surplus fund of $100,000, undivided profits of $34,110.05, and deposits of $536,788.79. The officers are E. T. Rowell, president; S. G. Mack, G. S. Motley, A. G. Cumnock, G. Ripley, J. B. Francis, J. Francis, J. Rogers, A. S. Lyon, W. S. Southworth, directors; F. P. Haggett, cashier.

The Lowell Trust Company is the latest addition to the city's banking facilities, whose doors were opened Feb. 9, 1891. It has a capital of $125,000. Hon. J. J. Donovan is president; Geo. T. Sheldon, treasurer; George M. Harrigan, actuary; and J. J. Hogan, J. W. Corcoran, C. O'Donnell, J. J. O'Donnell, J. A. Stiles, D. Wholey, D. Murphy, J. Marren, T. O'Brien, J. Crowley, D. Cole, R. Ripley, S. J. Johnson, W. J. Coughlin, T. C. Lee, C. H. Andrews, J. H. Coffey, C. H. Hanson, H. O'Sullivan are directors. The Trust Company is located in the new Donovan building at the junction of Central, Gorham and Middlesex streets, where it has already a thriving business.

## INSTITUTIONS FOR SAVINGS.

SIXTEEN MILLIONS OF DEPOSITS FLANKED BY SURPLUS MORE THAN A MILLION STRONG.

The savings banks of Lowell are widely celebrated for the remarkable number and character of their depositors and the enormous sums invested on behalf of their busy clients. Lowell has in its savings banks a larger sum, per capita of its total population, than any other city in the world. There are 44,699 open accounts, aggregating $16,108,544.12, or on an average of $360.38 to the credit of every account. This vast total represents a saving of more than two hundred dollars for every man, woman and child in the city; and when it is reflected that but one-half these people are employed in remunerative occupations, it will be seen that it represents an investment of more than four hundred dollars on the part of every working person in Lowell.

During the calendar year ending at the date of the latest return to the state commissioners, there were made 49,343 deposits, aggregating $3,113,673.22, an average of $63.10 for each entry, or an average addition of $69.66 to each account in the course of a year.

The Lowell Institution for Savings was incorporated in 1829, and has been known very generally as the "Old Lowell Savings Bank." For two years the Merrimack and Hamilton companies had acted as depositaries for the savings of their operatives, issuing books and paying interest, but when attention was called to the doubtful legality of such beneficence the plan was abandoned and a petition made to the legislature for a savings bank charter. Elisha Glidden was the first president, and

CENTRAL BLOCK.

he was succeeded in turn by Theodore Edson. John O. Green and Charles A. Savory. James G. Carney was the first treasurer, from 1829 to 1869; and his successor, the present incumbent, was his son. George J. Carney. The trustees are Geo. Motley, F. Nickerson, S. Kidder, A. B. French, F. Bailey, J. W. B. Shaw, F. Taylor, C. M. Fisk, D. B. Bartlett, A. St. John Chambre.

The City Institution for Savings organized in 1847, and has maintained its location ever since at the corner of Central and Hurd streets. Its first president was Rev. H. A. Miles, succeeded by Rev. D. C. Eddy, Dr. Nathan Allen and Hon. F. T. Greenhalge. John A. Buttrick, the first treasurer, was succeeded in 1875 by F. A. Buttrick, his son. The trustees are W. E. Livingston, C. R. Kimball, W. S. Bennett, A. Putnam, J. F. Howe, E. K. Perley, Percy Parker, L. Huntress, Frank Coburn, H. H. Barnes.

The Lowell Five Cent Savings Bank was incorporated in 1854. Rev. Horatio Wood was its first president, holding office until 1885, when, on his resignation, S. G. Mack was elected in his place. The first treasurer, A. S. Tyler, has filled the position since the organization of the bank. Hapgood Wright, J. F. Kimball, J. L. Cheney, G. F. Richardson, C. E. A. Bartlett, J. H. McAlvin, G. S. Cheney, A. C. Taylor, Dudley Foster, Charles Coburn, Arthur Staples, G. F. Penniman, A. C. Russell, W. S. Southworth, C. D. Palmer and F. P. Putnam are the present trustees. The bank occupies its elegant marble building at the corner of Merrimack and John streets. Its special field is the care of small deposits, being privileged to receive sums less than one dollar.

The Mechanics Savings Bank was organized in 1861, and its only presidents have been Wm. A. Burke and Jeremiah Clark. John F. Rogers was the first treasurer, succeeded by C. F. Battles and the present incumbent, C. C. Hutchinson. Until 1889 this bank was associated more or less closely with the Railroad National Bank in its quarters but since that date has occupied the second story of its own building on Merrimack street opposite Kirk street. Its present trustees are Jacob Rogers, Isaac Cooper, Ferdinand Rodliff, J. V. Keyes, A. G. Cumnock, C. L. Hildreth, John Davis, James Francis, W. W. Sherman, E. M. Tucke, J. G. Hill, W. D. Blanchard, J. G. Marshall, Francis

Carll, W. G. Ward, E. H. Cummings, E. N. Burke.

The Central Savings Bank was incorporated in 1871, and from the first Oliver H. Moulton has been its president. Its first treasurer was J. N. Pierce; but the present incumbent, Samuel A. Chase, has held the office since 1873. The trustees are F. Ayer, J. C. Abbott, E. B. Adams, E. Boyden, E. Brown, J. S. Brown, W. A. Brown, H. C. Church, R. Court, J. P. Folsom, P. C. Gates, J. R. Hayes, G. L. Huntoon, C. H. Latham, P. Lynch, A. S. Lyon, A. G. Pollard, A. Pratt, G. Runels, G. F. Scribner, D. Swan, B. Walker, S. N. Wood, G. W. Young. The bank has its place of business with the Merchants' National Bank, where is also maintained a safety-deposit vault.

The Merrimack River Savings Bank was also incorporated in 1871, and J. G. Peabody has been its president ever since. Its treasurers have been G. W. Knowlton, A. J. Flint and Nathan G. Lamson, the latter now holding the position. Its trustees are Samuel Horn, C. E. Paige, Francis Jewett, H. C. Howe, F. B. Shedd, A. D. Puffer, A. F. Wright, Charles Runels, C. J. Glidden, W. A. Ingham, P. P. Perham, J. C. Johnson, J. W. Bennett, Horace Ela, B. F. Sargent, C. F. Varnum, C. F. Young, G. W. Knowlton, C. E. Adams, Alfred Barney, R. G. Bartlett, S. B. Hall, Michael Corbett. Its banking rooms are at the corner of Middlesex and Thorndike streets, with the Wamesit National Bank.

The Lowell Co-Operative Bank was chartered April 29, 1885, with an authorized capital of $1,000,000, and it has been favored with continual prosperity. Twelve series of shares have been issued, and the latest dividend was at the rate of 7 per cent. The officers are A. B. Woodworth, president; S. R. Kitchen, vice-president; G. W. Batchelder, clerk; G. E. Metcalf, treasurer; J. L. Sedgley, L. Evans, Jr., E. G. Baker, J. O. Gulline, Thos. Collins, C. T. Rowland, C. L. Smith, L. F. Howard, S. J. Johnson, J. E. White, J. D. Hartwell, G. W. Brothers, F. Woodies, J. Murkland, S. A. Byam and E. S. Bickford, directors; G. H. Brown, L. F. Paulint, A. J. Murkland, auditors. Meetings are held the first Friday after the 10th of each month, at which the money on hand is loaned to the highest bidders. Last year the total receipts were $72,457,07.

FIVE CENT SAVINGS BANK BUILDING.

## REAL ESTATE.

THE SUBSTANTIAL BUSINESS DONE IN LOWELL WITHIN A YEAR.

($1,880,400 )

The above figures stand for the value of the bonafide real estate conveyances for the year ending May 1, 1891. There were in all 692 transactions, and when it is considered that the great majority of these were of a substantial and permanent character, some idea may be obtained of the progressive movement which is so rapidly developing the advantages our city offers.

A large per centage of these transactions represents the prosperity of individuals who have gratified the ambition to own their homes. Much of the conveyed lies on the lines of the street railway which have been recently opened or extended. The greatest number of such conveyances occur in Ward Four, proving the popularity of the Highlands for the purposes of residence. The increase in valuation in that district in 10 years, has been 109 per cent. Next comes Ward Two, embracing Centralville. With an increase of 73 per cent., Ward Three, which includes Ayers City, shows an increase of 60 per cent. Ward One, which contains the new municipal buildings, has increased 59 per cent. Ward Six follows with an increase of 53 per cent. Ward Five, including Pawtucketville, shows an increase of 46 per cent.

Now that the new boulevard has been laid out, it will throw some 300 acres of accessible residence land into the market in Ward Five.

The new postoffice building will have a beneficial effect upon the value of property in Wards Three and Four.

Of the 7900 acres of which Lowell is comprised, there are about 2000 acres which are both available and desirable for building purposes In the immediate vicinity of Lowell there are 10,000 acres which, in a very short time, will be treble the value at which they are at present held.

## INSURANCE.

For nineteen years the only insurance company in the city was the Lowell Mutual Fire Insurance Company, which was incorporated March 6, 1832, its first place of business being on the site of the present building of the Appleton Bank. The office was thence removed to the corner of Central and Market streets, where it remained forty years: in 1884 it was removed to the second story of the First National Bank block. Luther Lawrence was its first president, succeeded by Elisha Glidden, John Nesmith, Jona. Tyler, Horace Howard, J. B. French, J. H. B. Ayer, J. K. Fellows. Hon. J. C. Abbott, now president, has been in office since 1880, and E. T. Abbott, the secretary and treasurer, was elected in 1883. The directors are W. H. Wiggin, W. P. Brazer, C. A. Stott, W. E. Livingston, Benj. Walker, A. G. Pollard, P. C. Gates, F. A. Buttrick, C. W. Wilder, J. K. Fellows.

This company takes no risks outside the city of Lowell, and employs no agents. It had losses of but $3,029 last year. The amount of risks outstanding Jan. 1, 1891 was $3,591,871, with net assets of $70,902.99 and a permanent fund of $71,182.90. It pays return profits of 33 1-3, 50 and 70 per cent. on 1, 3 and 5 year policies.

The Traders and Mechanics Fire Insurance Company was incorporated in 1848 as a mutual company, to which a stock department was added in 1854. Both departments were conducted until 1881 when the capital and surplus were divided among the shareholders and the mutual business was continued. Levi Sprague is president and Edward M. Tucke is secretary; and the directors now are Jacob Rogers, C. C. Hutchinson, C. H. Coburn, G. F. Richardson, J. F. Kimball, H. C. Howe, F. P. Putnam. The gross assets Dec. 31, 1890 were $621,955.66, with liabilities of $234,463.39; leaving net assets of $387,192.27, of which $386,820.73 is a permanent fund. On the same date it had risks in force amounting to $30,668,025, and during the past year had losses of $55,778.75. This company pays 30, 50 and 70 per cent. return premiums on 1, 3 and 5-year policies.

Out-of-town insurance companies are represented in Lowell by Charles Coburn, H. C. Church & Son, G. W. Coburn & Son, J. B. Coleman, S. W. Cook, T. L. Dickey, J. M. Dixon, J. M. Kilgore, T. C. Lee, Metcalf & Hazen, N. W. Norcross & Co., F. W. Sherman, D. Walker, D. C. Wallace, J. B. Swift, C. W. Eaton, E. M. Tucke, E. T. Abbott, E. E. Mansur, F. M. Merrill and others.

## STREET RAILWAYS.

There have been no more prominent factors in the recent development of Lowell than the street railways. Statistics prove this beyond question of doubt.

The Lowell Horse Railroad company was organized in April, 1863, with an authorized capital of $100,000, and a paid up capital of $40,128.

On March 1, 1864, the lines were opened for business. There was a route from Belvidere to Pawtucket Falls, and one from the postoffice to Whipple's mills, via Central street. Later, the route on Bridge street was built, the line on Central street was changed to Gorham street, and a line laid through Middlesex street to the old Lafayette House. The latest extensions were on Westford and Chelmsford streets and Broadway.

The Lowell company enjoyed a monopoly of the carrying business until 1886, when the Lowell & Dracut company was organized under articles of association with a capital of $15,000. The line on Lakeview avenue was built and, after some opposition, the company obtained permission to lay tracks on Bridge street and enter the city proper.

In 1887, the company was chartered with a capital of $100,000, and at once

THE PROPOSED NEW HIGHLAND CLUB HOUSE.

issued $60,000 in bonds. The following May, the additional $40,000 was subscribed.

In 1889 bonds were issued for the purpose of making an electrical equipment for the line built to Lakeview. This has a total length of 5 miles, and conveys the people to the loveliest and best conducted Summer resort in New England.

In March, 1890, the railroad commissioners authorized the Lowell & Dracut company to issue further bonds for $100,000. At that time it had the routes running from the postoffice square to Pawtucketville, to Fort Hill Park, to the Lowell Cemetery and to Ward Four, in all 13$\frac{621}{1000}$ miles of track.

The Lowell company had at the same time 13$\frac{121}{1000}$ miles of track.

On the 20th of October, 1887, the directors of the Lowell & Dracut company acquired a controlling interest in the Lowell company.

It was soon found that the convenience of the public would be much enhanced and rapid transit virtually established, and the stockholders agreeing, consolidation was consummated and a new company organized under the title of the Lowell & Suburban Street Railway Company. The capital stock is placed at $300,000.

The company controls 27 miles of track, 75 per cent. of which is a tram rail of from 40 to 45 pounds, and the remainder the Providence girder and T rails. It owns 350 horses, which are sheltered in four stables located in Dracut at the city line, in East Merrimack street, in Middlesex street and in South Whipple street. It has 80 cars and 18 electric cars, and employs 300 men.

That the street railway is a factor in the development of the city is amply proved by the following statistics :

Percentage of increase of population, valuation and street railway facilities from 1880 to 1890.

| Assessors' Ward. | valuation. | Population. | St. Railway facilities. |
|---|---|---|---|
| 1 | 59 per cent. | 2.71 per cent. loss. | |
| 2 | 73 " | 46.07 " inc. | 291 per cent. |
| 3 | 60 " | 41.66 " " | 239 " |
| 4 | 109 " | 45.10 " " | 520 " |
| 5 | 40 " | 57.11 " " | 253 " |
| 6 | 53 " | 12.00 " " | Total, 3 miles |

There is an explanation of these figures. Ward One shows a loss of 2.71 per cent. in population, for the reason that the street railways afforded an opportunity for people to leave that congested district and put houses in other sections.

The figures of Ward Four are the most

significant—here, the increase of valuation was 109 per cent. ; the increase in population was only 45.10 per cent. while the increase in railway facilities was 520 per cent. It should be said that the increase in valuation is representative of the character of the houses built in this Ward. They are for the most part individual dwellings and the valuation is therefore of a very substantial character.

The increase in the population in Ward Five is larger than it is in any other Ward, while the increase in valuation is the lowest. This is accounted for by the fact that " Little Canada," with its great tenement blocks, offers cheap inducements for French Canadians to live there.

While the increase in population throughout the city has been 31 per cent. in ten years, the increase in dwelling houses has been 41 per cent. This has been possible through the medium of the street railway extensions, which have led people to go toward the suburbs and own their own homes. From 1880 to 1885 the population increased 7 per cent ; street railway facilities increased in the same period, 20 per cent.

From 1885 to 1890, the increase of population was 21 per cent. : for the same period the increase in street railway facilities was 400 per cent., a most remarkable progress, which proves the wisdom of the enterprise which gave the city the railway routes it now enjoys. And that it has been a profitable investment may be gathered from the fact that while the population increased 21 per cent from 1885 to 1890, the income of the street railway companies increased 300 per cent. in the same period.

### THE NEW COMPANY.

The Lowell & Suburban Street railway company is the outcome of the consolidation of the two companies. Its officers are : E. M. Tucke, president ; August Fels, vice-president ; Percy Parker, treasurer ; P. F. Sullivan, secretary ; directors E. M. Tucke, A. Fels, P. Parker, P. F. Sullivan, T. Costello, E. A. Smith, W. M. Sawyer, F. W. Howe, S. Bachman, M. F. Brennan and J. Lennon, and its capital stock is $300,000. It has adopted plans for the development of the service which will ultimately involve an outlay of $1,000,000. These plans are justified by the needs of the community and by the constantly growing demand for extended service.

The board of aldermen have given the company license to double its tracks in all streets where they are now laid, to extend its tracks to the city line and also to set up poles and maintain an electrical equipment. These are great privileges and the company is preparing to make the most of its advantage.

The Lowell & Dracut Company was one of the first in the state to adopt electricity as a motive power. It ran its first cars by that force, August 1, 1889. It had then eight cars, it now has eighteen fitted with motors. Its success, its economy and great utility have united to induce the directors of the new road to adopt electricity for the entire street railway system.

The plans for a power station have been prepared. The building will be located at the corner of Middlesex and Pawtucket streets and will contain a plant of 2,000 horse power. That, with an average of 20 horse power to a car, will supply motive energy for 100 cars.

With this building will be constructed a car house and repair shops. A short spur track will bring coal from the adjoining railroad into the boiler house and all material needed for equipment.

All the tracks on the main lines will be doubled. Under the present system the cars run on 15 minute time; when the tracks are doubled it will be possible to run on shorter time and give the public a much more rapid service. It will cost $200,000 to double the tracks and make the proposed extensions. These are from the Bridge street terminus to the "Yellow meeting house" in Dracut; from the Middlesex street terminus through Middlesex village to North Chelmsford; from the Chelmsford street terminus to Chelmsford centre; from the Gorham street terminus to North Billerica, and from the Nesmith street terminus to Phenix.

Thus will all the manufacturing suburbs be brought into closer unity with the city, and the people in the denser quarters will be invited to the occupancy of the land that lies between those villages and the city, these extensions will add much to the valuation of the city, for the most distant point will be within 15 minutes ride of the business centre.

## RAILROAD FACILITIES.

Lowell enjoys exceptional railroad facilities. The Boston & Lowell railroad was projected by Patrick T. Jackson, the founder of our cotton industry, and completed in 1834. It was one of the earliest railroads in the United States.

The Lowell & Nashua railroad was subsequently built and then followed the Stonybrook railroad, the Framingham railroad, the Salem railroad, and the Andover railroad.

Lowell is connected with a system which furnishes transportation to every section of the country. With the exception of the Framingham railroad, all the roads entering Lowell are now part of the Boston & Maine system.

The Boston & Lowell railroad, or the southern division of the Boston & Maine, is 26 miles in length. Its terminus in Lowell is at the Merrimack street station. It has direct connections with the Lowell & Nashua, the Stonybrook, the Rochester, the Concord, the Northern, the Worcester, Nashua & Portland, the Montpelier &

Wells River, the Vermont Central, the Passumpsic, the Claremont & Peterboro, the Concord & Montreal and the Canadian Pacific railroads. Goods are now shipped direct from our mill yards to the Pacific Coast for China and Japan. Lowell is on the direct line of travel to Canada and the White Mountains.

The Stonybrook railroad runs from North Chelmsford to Ayer Junction making connections with the Fitchburg and the Worcester and Nashua railroads.

The Lowell and Salem railroad connects Lowell with that port and the intervening cities and towns.

The Lowell and Andover railroad has its terminus in the Central Street Station. It is a branch of the Northern Division of the Boston and Maine railroad, having direct communication with Newburyport, and the coast towns lying between that city and Portland, Me. At Portland it makes close connections with the Portland and Ogdensburgh, the Maine Central and the Grand Trunk railroads.

The Framingham is a branch of the Old Colony, running from South Framingham to Lowell. It is a direct line to Fall River, Providence and New York from which places there are two through trains every day.

There are three stations in Lowell, one in Central street, one in Merrimack street and one in Middlesex street: the latter is the principal station, and among the improvements contemplated by Manager Furber, are a handsome and more commodious building to replace a structure which is both out of date and hopelessly inadequate to accomodate the public.

The company has made many recent changes in the freight department. It has acquired much land in the neighborhood of the Middlesex street station and on the line of Gorham street has built several spacious freight sheds. These, in addition to the freight yards in Western avenue, the yards of the Lowell and Andover railroad and the newly acquired yards near the Concord river, will enable the railroad company to give our local trade a prompt, convenient and efficient service.

The city is a net-work of spur tracks running from the main lines to the mill yards. The Framingham road also has a spur line running to the industries in Ayer city. On all these numerous lines of railroad there is more or less land that is desirable for manufacturing purposes. The tariff rates are not high and the service is accomodatingly frequent.

There are 23 trains from Boston on the Southern division, every day, and 12 on the Western division, a total of 35 trains a day from the capital. The number of trains from Lowell to Boston on the Southern division, is 23 and on the Western division, 13. There are in all 71 trains in the daily service between Boston and Lowell.

There are three daily express trains to and from Montreal and an equal number in the White Mountains service during the summer season. There are six daily trains to and from Salem ; 36 daily trains between Lowell and Lawrence, and 20 daily trains between Lowell and Haverhill.

The improvements which are contemplated at the Middlesex street station will be commenced as soon as the vexed question of grade crossings is definitely settled.

## RESIDENTIAL.

### THE SEVERAL SECTIONS OF THE CITY WHERE THE PEOPLE LIVE.

Lowell is most attractively located and the home sections of the city have each a distinctive name. They are Belvidere, Oaklands, Centralville, the Highlands and Pawtucketville.

#### BELVIDERE.

Belvidere is built upon a hill and is one of the most beautiful sections of the city. It is here that ex-Governor Butler lives, and his house has a most charming view of the river as it rushes under the Centralville heights over the rocky bed of Hunt's falls. Nesmith street, named after the late John Nesmith, at one time lieutenant-governor of the state, is a beautiful thoroughfare, shaded with fine trees. At the farther end of this street is the Rogers Fort Hill Park, 200 feet above the level of the city. Andover street runs along the heights above the river and is lined with beautiful residences. The neighborhood of Park Garden is peaceful and picturesque and there are many fine old residences in that vicinity.

#### OAKLANDS.

Oaklands is a recently opened territory in the region of Belvidere, one of the most attractive of the several residential sections of the city. The territory comprises 165 acres, and is the property of a syndicate consisting of Messrs. Shepard, Russell & Fuller. The larger part of this territory is situated in Lowell ; the rest lies in the town of Tewksbury.

Fort Hill Park is 200 feet high. It commands an extensive view of the surrounding country. Lying to the east of the park are two other eminences of similar height. One of these is Belvidere, the other is Oaklands. Oaklands begins in the valley behind the elevation of Belvidere, and extends upward until it reaches a parallel height and overlooks the residence of Gen. Butler.

Here, the view is superb, bounded by the horizon 29 miles distant. On a clear night, the light at Minot's Ledge can be distinctly discerned. Lawrence, the Readings, Danvers and Somerville are in sight,

·ODD·FELLOWS·BUILDING·
·LOWELL MASS·
MERRILL & CUTLER ARCHTS
LOWELL MASS

and Tewksbury and Andover are part of the panorama which makes this section so delightful. To the north, glimpses may be obtained of the New Hampshire hills, and to the south lie the Chelmsfords with their dense woods and the Billericas with their spires and gleaming fields. Two rivers are in sight, the picturesque Merrimack wending eastward to Lawrence and the sea, and the classic Concord meandering through the meadows of Billerica. At this elevation the air is cool even in the fervency of summer, and the hill of Belvidere breaks the winter wind before it reaches Oaklands.

The land is a clayey gravel which makes excellent roads and affords dry and comfortable building sites. Formerly, the hill was covered with a heavy growth of oak, but now it has been stripped with a judicious selection of much of the timber. There are shady groves here and there, and wherever it has been possible to spare a tree on the line of the avenues it has been spared.

At the crest of the hill, at what was once the Hovey farm, there is a crescent partially laid out, upon what it was the late Mr. Hovey's ambition to see an Episcopal college established. The present owners, in laying out Holyrood avenue will follow the lines laid down by Mr. Hovey, marked by him with a row of elms.

On the brow of the hill are two acres of land preserved by Mr. Hovey's will, for the accommodation of an Episcopal church.

This territory is traversed by avenues 50 feet wide and by cross streets. Hanover avenue goes, straight as crows fly, from Andover street to the Boston & Lowell railroad tracks, is a mile and a half long. Park View avenue lies parallel and further up the hill.

There are 450 lots, averaging 6000 square feet each, on this hill territory, and of that number 150 have been sold. A number of beautiful residences have been erected. Many more are in course of construction. The streets are under municipal control, and gas and city water are accommodations enjoyed by everybody. There is a fifteen-minute-horse-car service and the post-office is only 15 minutes' distant.

## CENTRALVILLE.

Centralville lies on the north side of the Merrimack river. It is reached by two magnificent iron bridges over which the street railways pass. The heights of Centralville, on the summit of which the city reservoirs are located, rise 200 feet above the level of the river. They command a fine view of the lower city, of the surrounding country and the mountains to the north and west.

It is one of the most favored home sections of the city. There are some rare old houses there which stand monuments to the good taste, the comfort and the hospitality of the early settlers. The Parker, Hildreth, Tucke and McEvoy houses are types of the early day.

On the lower grounds of Centralville the land is level until it reaches the neighborhood of Crescent hill. Here it rises again, and again the character of the houses change; for while on the low land the tenements prevail, in the highlands the individual dwelling is the rule. The streets are finely shaded with rare old trees.

## THE HIGHLANDS.

Twenty years ago, the Highlands was a farming district. There were oak and pine woods upon it fifteen years ago. It is now one of the great residence sections of the city. People who live in the Highlands would not live anywhere else; they say the section excels Belvidere and perhaps it will when its trees have cast more shade than they do now, for the streets and thoroughfares are none of them more than 15 years old. The houses here are well separated and green lawns and shady gardens are everywhere the rule. Building operations are very lively in this district; and the men who reside here have recently founded a club and will build a club house of generous dimensions upon a sightly eminence.

## PAWTUCKETVILLE.

This delightful section has but recently been opened up to general occupation. It is on the north side of the Merrimack, and through it the river tumbles in the picturesque and rugged beauty of Pawtucket rapids. The rapids are spanned by a substantial iron bridge from which the view of the falls is one of the most attractive in the city.

The city authorities have laid out a magnificent boulevard along the river bank in this section, and the improvement will bring a great deal of very desirable land into the market. There are some fine residences in this quarter, among them those of Miss Lucy Fay and A. C. Varnum.

The land lying between Varnum avenue and the boulevard is owned by Daniel Gage, Lucy Fay, William H. Hill, heirs of Willard Coburn, Mrs. C. A. Green, J. M. Wilson, Dr. Geo. Clement, T. J. Underwood, Geo. L. Goodale, Edward S. Howe. The tract contains from 250 to 300 acres.

## LOWELL'S EXCEPTIONAL PRIVILEGE IN CHEAP ILLUMINATION.

A large share of the city's artificial light is still supplied by the Lowell Gas Light company. This company was incorporated in 1849 with a capital of $500,000. Its extensive plant is located on School street near the tracks of the Nashua & Lowell Railroad.

The annual consumption of coal by this company reaches over 20,000 tons, from which are produced 215,000,000 cubic feet of illuminating gas of excellent quality. The gas service of the city is furnished through nearly seventy-five miles of mains reaching well into the remote residential districts. The exceedingly low price at which the company has been able to furnish gas and still earn for its stockholders handsome dividends, has brought it about that the question of municipal lighting has so far possessed but little interest for Lowell.

The figures of the table which follows, made up from the average price per thousand at which gas was furnished in the principal cities and towns in Massachusetts during the year 1889-90, will seem to show that Lowell easily leads all her sister cities in this respect. Contrary to the usual practice, the Lowell company has but one price, alike for both large and small consumer. With the liberal discount of 20 per cent. for prompt payment, Lowell's gas easily leads the list.

| Lowell | | | | | $1.10 |
|---|---|---|---|---|---|
| Boston | - | - | - | - | 1.23 |
| Brocton | - | - | - | - | 2.09 |
| Cambridge - | - | - | - | - | 1.67 |
| Chelsea | - | - | - | - | 1.96 |
| Fall River - | - | - | - | - | 1.57 |
| Fitchburg - | - | - | - | - | 1.92 |
| Gloucester - | - | - | - | - | 1.81 |
| Haverhill - | - | - | - | - | 1.40 |
| Holyoke | - | - | - | - | 1.58 |
| Ipswich | - | - | - | - | 3.01 |
| Jamaica Plain | - | - | - | - | 2.00 |
| Lawrence - | - | - | - | - | 1.41 |
| Lynn | - | - | - | - | 1.76 |
| Malden | - | - | - | - | 1.95 |
| New Bedford | - | - | - | - | 1.52 |
| Newburyport | - | - | - | - | 2.01 |
| Salem | - | - | - | - | 1.80 |
| Springfield - | - | - | - | - | 1.68 |
| Waltham | - | - | - | - | 1.80 |
| Woburn | - | - | - | - | 1.78 |
| Worcester - | - | - | - | - | 1.50 |

The officers of the company are Sewall G. Mack, president; Jacob Rogers, treasurer; D. B. Bartlett, clerk; Sewell G. Mack, Jacob Rogers, James B. Francis, Levi Sprague and John F. Kimball, directors.

## ELECTRICITY.

### ONE OF THE BEST EQUIPPED PLANTS IN NEW ENGLAND FOR LIGHTING AND POWER.

The artificial illumination of Lowell, aside from the gas and gasoline lights—the latter in the suburbs only—rests entirely with one large and flourishing body, the Lowell Electric Light Corporation. It is a body which first organized on a small scale and gradually extended its scope so as to entirely control the business of lighting our streets, places of business and even homes, with electricity. The corporation is purely of local origin and Lowell men still control and guide its fortunes. It first organized in 1881 under state laws, with a capital of $10,000, commencing with two Weston arc light machines, and, leasing power from an accommodating saw mill.

A year later, the Middlesex Electric Light Company was formed and established a small plant on Middle street. The Thomson Houston system was introduced, and a little later the latter company bought out the Weston Company.

The business increased as the demand for electric lighting became general, and the Middle street plant became one of no mean proportions. Two years ago, the company reorganized under the name it now bears. Steps were taken to secure a site for a plant which would fully meet

ELECTRIC LIGHT STATION.

future requirements. A site was secured on the line of Boston and Maine railroad, in Belvidere and operations commenced.

The new station on Perry street, completed and occupied about Feb. 1, 1891, is designed for 3000 h. p. There is a main building of two stories in height, with a large boiler room adjoining the easterly end, and a coal shed capable of holding a thousand tons of fuel. The boiler room is 66x96 feet with accommodations for 16 horizontal tubular boilers 72 inches in diameter, 17 feet long, each containing 140 three inch tubes, built by Scannell and Wholley of this city. The boilers are in two rows and between them are the smoke flues entering a chimney 175 feet high with a 7 foot bore. All pipes from the boilers to adjuncts are of brass; the steam pipes vary from 5 to 14 inches in diameter. The feeding sources are one each of Knowles and Worthington pumps and Hancock inspirator.

The engine room in the main part is 140x45 feet, on the second story, and it contains at present one 250 h. p. cross compound Harris-Corliss engine with cylinders 8x30 inches with 36 inch stroke; one 200 h. p. Atlas engine of high pressure; one 500 h. p. tandem compound Harris-Corliss engine with cylinders 22.440 inches and 48 inch stroke; also a 300 h. p. cross compound condensing engine. There is space for two more engines of large capacity.

The engines are set on heavy granite foundations. Under the engine room there are two Knowles condensers for the Corliss engines, a Harris condenser; an air pump; a 500 h. p. national feed water heater and two smaller heaters. On the ground level on the other side of the building is the shafting room containing the best set line of shafting in New England. The foundations are of Conway granite resting on a 12 inch bed of concrete made of broken stone and cement. The main journal bearings are supported on solid granite stands. The main pulley driven from the 500 h. p. engine is 72 inches in diameter by 52 inches face. The belt passes under an idler or belt tightener. Two eclipse clutches 48 and 50 inches in diameter are on the journal. Other clutches subdivide the line of shafting.

The dynamo room is overhead and contains 13 50-light Thomson-Houston arc light dynamos, two 50 h. p. 500 volt Thomson-Houston generators for stationary motors, four 100 h. p. Bentley-Knight railway generators, two 1300 light and one 1000 light alternating incandescent dynamos.

The station is wired with okonite and the switch boards and appurtenances are of the very latest and best adapted styles.

The entire construction of the building is of the heaviest and most substantial kind and the Lowell station is probably the best appointed in New England.

The plant is to be increased in size and the capabilities for furnishing electrical motive and illuminating power to be developed to the utmost. The corporation has quite recently taken hold of the Eddy motor, pronounced to be among the best in use, and as sale agents and introducers of it in this section, will use it in connection with the plant. The corporation sell the motors outright in sizes from 1-8 to 40 h. p. and are able to supply the necessary current to run them in any part of the city. To this fact they call particular attention, believing that small and independent industries may be established in many sections of the city, for which the power may be furnished through the joint medium of an Eddy motor and an electrical current.

The officers of the company are George W. Fifield, president; William A. Ingham, vice president; John H. McAlvin, treasurer and secretary; L. I. Fletcher, manager; directors, G. W. Fifield, W. A. Ingham, J. H. McAlvin, L. I. Fletcher, Lowell, Jas. H. Tolles, Charles F. Collins, Nashua, N. H., Cyrus Conant, Concord, Mass.

:Lowell·Cricket·Club·Proposed·Pavilion:
ARNOLD ? SPALER ARCHITECT LOWELL

## LOWELL'S TELEPHONE SYSTEM.

The first record of a petition for leave to erect wires on buildings and on poles for the construction of a telephone system in Lowell came from the New England Telephone Company, March 12, 1878, and was signed by Charles J. Glidden. It was referred to the Committee on Lands and Buildings of the City Council, March 26th of that year, the committee consisting of H. R. Barker, George F. Scribner, Charles H. Harvey, Robert Goulding and Samuel D. Butterworth, reported in favor of the petition and the petition was granted.

It does not follow, however, that the New England Telephone Company was the first to do business in Lowell. William H. Bent, who was interested in the formation of the early telephone companies believes the Pioneer Telephone Company, doing business between this city and Boston was the first company in the field, and that the Lowell Telephone Exchange was the first to accommodate the public. Others say Providence, R. I., opened a telephone exchange about the same time as Lowell.

According to a resident familiar with the business, the Lowell District Tele-phone Company was organized in 1879, with a capital of $15,000. The rapid development of the use of the telephone was shown by an advertisement of this company in 1880. in which it was asserted that the company had 500 stations in Lowell and 1000 in Boston and suburbs. The Lowell central office was then at Room 12, Shattuck's block, W. A. Ingham was president and Charles J. Glidden, treasurer and manager.

In 1880, consolidation of the Lowell District Telephone Company was perfected with the Worcester Company, and afterward with the National Bell Company of Maine, under the name of the Lowell District Telephone Company. The capital stock of the new company was $1,500,-000.

In October, 1883, the consolidation of the National Bell of Maine Company, the Granite State, Boston & Northern, Bay State, Suburban and Lowell District Telephone Companies, was consummated in what is now known as the New England Telephone Company. The capital of the new company was $12,000,000. The officers of that company are: Thomas Sherwin, president; H. S. Hyde, vice-president; W. R. Driver, treasurer; S. W. Leedom, secretary and auditor; J. N. Keller, general manager. J. W. Duxbury is superintendent of District No. 1, which includes Lowell.

W. H. Lincoln is manager of the Lowell exchange of the company. There are 802 subscribers in the Lowell exchange, and in addition to the many miles of line which cover the city and surrounding towns, the company has 13 ex-territorial lines, allowing communication with all the cities and towns in its territory having subscribers. Miss Nellie Hines is the chief operator, and ten assistants answer the hundreds of calls in the day and evening.

Of the many citizens who were interested in the organization of the first telephone companies, William A. Ingham,

Charles J. Glidden, A. A. Coburn, Loren N. Downs and William H. Bent were the best known.

They also aided in establishing the Erie Telephone Company, which has territory in Ohio, Texas, Arkansas, Minnesota and Dakota. Levi Sprague is president of the Erie company at present, and Charles J. Glidden. Francis Jewett, A. C. Russell, A. S. Adams, C. E. Adams and J. W. C. Pickering are directors. Charles J. Glidden is secretary and treasurer.

Frederick Ayer, Dr. M. G. Parker and other Lowell citizens are large holders of New England Company's stock.

Lowell citizens also largely aided in establishing the Union Telegraph and Telephone Company of Northern New York, and own considerable stock of the company at present.

## INCORPORATED INDUSTRIES.

MILLIONS OF DOLLARS AND THOUSANDS OF PEOPLE WORKING TOGETHER FOR GOOD.

There are in Lowell 42 companies chartered under the laws of the State, whose aggregate capital is $18,218,000, and whose combined assets are $34,628,261. These figures do not include the hundred private establishments whose millions of capital and assets are not available for statistics, since they make no returns to the authorities of the Commonwealth.

No other city has a greater number and variety of industries, as no other city has so large a proportion of its total population employed in remunerative occupations from day to day. Therein is the remarkable strength and staying power of the city, which has maintained a steady and uniform growth, albeit a rapid one, and which promises so much for its future development.

Some idea of the people thus employed may be gleaned from the figures quoted below. Beside the incorporated industries of the city all other industries of any importance are given:

Cotton mills, Merrimack Company, incorporated 1822; capital stock, $2,500,000; number of spindles, 156,480; number of looms, 4607; employ 3000 hands; Joseph S. Ludlam, agent.

Hamilton Company, incorporated 1825; capital stock, $1,800,000; number of spindles, 109,816; number of looms,

3030; employ 1850 hands; O. H. Moulton, agent.

Appleton Company, incorporated 1828; capital stock, $600,000; number of spindles, 50,776; number of looms, 1639, employ 825 hands; C. H. Richardson, agent.

Lawrence Company, incorporated 1831; capital stock, $1,500,000; number of spindles, 120,000; number of looms, 3432; employ 3140 hands; John Kilburn, agent.

Boott Company, incorporated 1835; capital stock, $1,200,000; number of spindles, 151,192; number of looms, 4139; employ 2210 hands; Alexander G. Cumnock, agent.

Massachusetts Company, incorporated 1839; capital stock, $1,800,000; number of spindles, 126,648; number of looms, 3905; employ 1800 hands; William S. Southworth, agent.

Tremont and Suffolk Company, incorporated as two companies in 1831, consolidated in 1871; capital stock, $1,200,000; number of spindles, 114,000; number of looms, 3900; employ 2000 hands; Edward W. Thomas, agent.

Woolen Mills, Lowell Manufacturing Company, incorporated 1828; capital stock, $2,000,000; number of spindles, 24,750; number of looms, 385; employ 2100 hands; A. S. Lyon, superintendent.

Middlesex Company, incorporated 1830; capital stock, $750.000; number of spindles, 18,640; number of looms, 200; employ 700 hands; Oliver H. Perry, agent.

Lowell Machine Shop, incorporated 1845; capital stock, $900,000; employ 1500 hands; Charles L. Hildreth, superintendent.

Lowell Bleachery and Dye Works, incorporated 1832; capital stock, $400,0 0; employ 262 hands; James N. Bourne, agent.

New England Bunting Company, runs 70 looms; employ 75 hands; E. S. Hylan, manager.

United States Bunting Company, has 5000 spindles and 250 looms; employ 700 hands; Walter H. McDaniels, manager.

Belvidere Woolen Company, employ 250 hands; Charles A. Stott, agent.

L. W. Faulkner & Sons, manufacturers of dress goods, flannels and gents' suitings; employ 500 hands.

Stirling Flannel Mills, employ 135 hands; E. D. Holden, agent.

Crossley Company, flannels, dress goods and cloakings; employ 100 hands.

W. H. Carter, dress goods; employs 50 hands.

United States Cord Company, employ 15 hands.

Cutter & Walker Company, suspenders, shoe linings, etc.; employ 30 hands.

Lowell Goring Works; employ 12 hands.

Novelty Suspender Works; employ 35 hands.

Thorndike Manufacturing Company, suspenders; employ 150 hands.

W. L. Davis, manufacturer of webbing; employs 15 hands.

Lowell Hosiery Company; employ 300 hands.

Shaw Stocking Company; employ 500 hands; George L. Hooper, manager.

Brown's Hosiery; employs 13 hands.

Criterion Knitting Company, jersey vests; employ 15 hands.

Pickering Knitting Company, men's underwear; employ 200 hands.

Excelsior Knitting Works, jersey underwear; employ 15 hands.

Sugden Bagging Company; employ 5 hands.

Samuel G. Cooper, and Parsons & Mealey, copper stamps and stencils; employ 6 hands each.

Lladnek Print and Dye Works; employ 60 hands.

Walsh Worsted Mills; employ 150 hands.

Lowell Worsted Mills; employ 90 hands.

John M. Pevey, cotton yarns; employs 100 hands.

Whittier Cotton Mills, yarns, twines, etc.; employ 75 hands.

M. & B. Rhodes, worsted yarns; employ 13 hands.

Josiah Gates & Sons, belting, etc.; employ 30 hands.

Whiting & Weston, belting; employ 8 hands.

Wm. H. Parker & Sons, bobbins, spools, etc.; employ 200 hands.

John L. Cheney & Co., bobbins, spools and shuttles; employ 75 hands.

Samuel E. & T. Stott, card clothing, wool combs, etc.; employ 50 hands.

W. H. Bagshaw, card clothing, card pins, etc.; employs 25 hands.

Lowell Card Company; employ 22 hands.

Amraytoon Paper Tube Company, employs 25 hands. Cop tubes also manufactured by Haworth & Watson, Acme Company and Conical Cop Tube Company.

George W. Harris, loom harnesses; employs 35 hands.

D. C. Brown, loom harnesses and reeds; employs 30 hands.

John Tripp & Company, roll coverings; employ 16 hands.

Coburn Shuttle Company; employ 40 hands.

Jaques Shuttle Company; employ 35 hands.

Lowell Steam Boiler Works; employ from 40 to 70 hands.

Scannell & Wholey, steam boilers, etc.; employ 40 hands.

James A. Ready, boilers, fire escapes, etc.; employs 15 hands.

American Bolt Company; employs 150 hands.

United States Cartridge Company; employs 200 hands.

Dougherty Bros., iron and brass founders; employ 75 hands. A. F. Nichols, 50 hands. Pevey Bros., 70 hands. Union Iron Foundry, 40 hands.

Daniel Lovejoy & Sons, machine knives; employ 25 hands.

D. H. Wilson & Company, copper work; employ 17 hands.

APPLETON BLOCK, CENTRAL STREET.

W. A. Mack & Company and Daniel Cushing & Company, galvanized iron workers; employ 18 hands each.

George L. Cady and Cyrus Perkins, machinists' tools; employ 10 and 5 hands respectively.

W. W. Carey, wood-working machinery; employs 50 hands.

Middlesex Machine Company; employ 18 hands.

J. Clark, cotton machinery; employs 18 hands.

George W. Fifield, machinists' tools; employs 60 hands.

Kitson Machine Company; employ 225 hands.

Lowell Tool and Engine Company; employ 20 hands.

F. S. Perkins, lathes and machinists' tools; employs from 50 to 75 hands.

A. L. Wright, engine lathes; employs 30 hands.

Knowles Scale Works; employ 12 hands.

Lowell Scale Company; employ 6 hands.

Swain Turbine and Manufacturing Company, work done by contract.

American Wire Goods Company; employ 30 hands.

Rice & Company, wire goods; employ 50 hands.

Woods, Sherwood & Company, wire goods and plating; employ 75 hands.

Otis Allen & Son, wooden boxes; employ 100 hands.

A. L. Brooks & Company, packing cases and mouldings; employ 55 hands.

Davis & Sargent, boxes; employ 45 hands.

Allen & Thompson, boxes; employ 25 hands.

A. Bachelder & Company, bungs and plugs; employ 10 hands.

Lamson Consolidated Store Service Company; employ 330 hands.

A. P. Bateman, doors, sashes, etc.; employs 30 hands.

S. W. Fletcher, doors, window frames, etc.; employs 30 hands.

Wm. Kelly & Son, doors, blinds, etc.; employ 20 hands.

J. G. Peabody & Sons, doors and sashes; employ 30 hands.

Amasa Pratt & Company, doors, etc.; employ 50 hands.

Marshall & Crosby, furniture; employ 40 hands.

John Welch, furniture; employs 20 hands.

C. I. Taylor & Company, furniture; employ 17 hands.

Mark Holmes, Jr. & Son, house finish; employ 10 hands.

Middlesex Friction Match Company; employ 50 hands.

G. W. Bagley and R. J. Colcord, refrigerators; employ 15 hands each.

Merrimack Croquet Company; employ about 60 hands.

John Pilling, boots and shoes; employs 140 hands.

J. M. Storer, boots and shoes; employs 80 hands.

F. E. Jewett & Company, cider vinegar; employ 25 hands.

Bacheller, Dumas & Company, book binding; employ 20 hands.

Fay Bros. & Hosford, carriages, sleighs, etc.; employ 14 hands.

Sawyer Carriage Company; employ 22 hands. Other manufacturers are J. H. Swett, E. P. Bryant, and G. F. Hill.

C. A. Kendall, cement pipes; employs 10 hands.

Lowell Felting Mills; employ 20 hands.

Andrews & Wheeler, marble and stone work; employ 25 hands. Other stone workers are L. D. Gumb, C. C. Laurin, Wm. Andrews, James Mahan, Charles Runels and T. H. Spencer.

E. Hapgood & Son, mattresses; employ 35 hands.

L. W. Hawkes & Company, furniture and mattresses; employ 12 hands.

W. H. Hope & Company, milled machine screws, etc.; employ 15 hands.

C. F. Hatch & Company, paper boxes; employ from 80 to 100 hands.

Charles Littlefield & Company, paper boxes; employ 40 hands.

E. W. Hoyt & Company, cologne; employ 25 hands.

Novelty Plaster Works; employ 30 hands.

J. C. Ayer Company, medicines; employ 318 hands.

C. I. Hood & Company, medicines; employ 275 hands.

Moxie Nerve Food Company; employ 50 hands.

Arey, Maddock & Locke, tanning and currying; employ from 125 to 150 hands.

White Bros. & Company, leather manufacturers; employ 250 hands.

W. H. Carter, wool scourer; employs 56 hands.

# MANUFACTURING SUBURBS.

## THE BUSY VILLAGES THAT SURROUND, AND MAKE THEIR MARKET IN LOWELL.

There are in the immediate vicinity of Lowell, five villages or settlements, built and maintained by the industries there established. They are North Billerica, North Chelmsford, Collinsville, Navy Yard and Phoenix. The people employed in these industries spend their earnings in Lowell.

### NORTH BILLERICA.

The village of North Billerica is situated on the banks of the Concord River—four miles from Lowell. It has a population of 1000 and three flourishing industries. It was here that the late Gov. Talbot resided, and the village owes much of its prosperous comfort to his generous care. Mrs. Talbot, his widow, has just had constructed a beautiful memorial hall for the use of the people of the town. The town hall was recently destroyed by fire, but plans have been prepared for the building of a new one.

There are three churches in the village, Baptist, Episcopal and Catholic. The first was built by Gov. Talbot; the Talbot heirs gave the land for the second, and the third has had much substantial assistance from the Talbot family.

There is a well provided library connected with the Talbot mills; and the Father Mathew Temperance Institute has quite recently erected a very fine building on land given it by the Talbots.

The Talbot school is a modern building containing graded schools. There is a fire company in the village, and an appropriation has recently been made for the purchase of a steam fire engine.

The taxes are $10 per $1000.

The Concord River furnishes an average of 500 horse power.

The Talbot mills manufacture dress goods, flannels and carriage cloths, 3,000,-000 yards a year. They employ 275 hands, and the volume of their business is $1,500,000 a year. The officers are Solomon Lincoln, president; F. S. Clark, treasurer, and James Stott, superintendent.

The Faulkner Manufacturing Company makes flannels, and employs 90 hands. The volume of business is about $1,000,-

000 a year, and the number of yards manufactured 1,090,000.

Talbot Dyewood & Chemical Company, manufactures nitric, muriatic and sulphuric acids, oil vitriol, blue vitriol and other manufacturing chemicals. It employs 30 men, and the yearly volume of business will reach $500,000. The officers are J. D. Gould, president; James F. Preston, treasurer. The Company has an office and store at No. 24 Middle street, Lowell.

### DRACUT.

That portion of Dracut lying on Beaver Brook near its confluence with the Merrimack River, is known as the "Navy Yard." It must have been a local wag who so christened it, for the only navy in that vicinity is composed of a few old dorys and flat-bottomed boats. The village is but a short distance from the city line, and is reached by the electric cars, which run to Lake Mascuppic.

Beaver Brook furnishes 100 horse power.

The Merrimack woollen mills, manufacture 144,000 yards of cloakings, 48,000 yards of dress goods and 96,000 shawls per annum, and employs 450 hands. The volume of business for a year is $2,000,000. The mills are owned by Solomon Bachman, No. 87 Worth street, New York; the present agent is August Fels.

Parker & Bassett manufacture 5000 pounds of paper and employ 15 men. Their business will average $150,000 a year.

At Collinsville, further up the brook, there is quite a settlement clustered about the mills belonging to Michael Collins. These employ 260 hands and manufacture 228,000 yards of heavy woollens per annum. The volume of business is close to $1,500,000.

### CHELMSFORD.

West, beyond Middlesex Village, lies the thriving village of North Chelmsford. Its industries are important and afford employment to 500 people. It is the terminus of the Stonybrook railroad running to Ayer Junction, and is on the line of the

Lowell and Nashua railroad. The Stony-brook furnishes 200 horse power. There is no finer or more desirable place for the location of industries. It is within ten minutes ride on the railroad of the centre of the city and it is the purpose of the Street Railway Company to extend its electric line to that village. In addition to Stonybrook, there is another stream, Day's brook, which guarantees a constant supply of water, and which at one time furnished the motive power for Swain's Turbine works. Since the discontinuance of those works the water runs unused to the river.

There are many acres of desirable land available for manufacturing purposes along the lines of the Lowell and Nashua and Stonybrook railroads, along the banks of the river and the brooks, and on the shores of Leach's pond, a considerable body of water which is used to augment the power furnished by the Stonybrook.

The taxes of the town are $8.50 on $1000, and the advantages are almost identical to those enjoyed by the adjoining city.

The industries are, George C. Moore's extensive wool scouring and worsted yarn mills. He employs 250 hands and turns over 4,000,000 pounds of wool a year.

The Chelmsford Foundry Company, with office at 131 Portland street, Boston, was established in 1822. The president and treasurer is G. T. Sheldon, E. D. Bearce is the present superintendent. The Company manufactures 4500 tons of iron per annum into columns and beams and employs 150 men.

The Silver and Gay Machine Works give employment to 50 men and manufacture all kinds of machinery.

There are several granite cutters and carriage builders in the neighborhood.

There are two churches in the village, and the school accommodations are ample.

There are two small manufacturing concerns in Chelmsford Centre, which employ 30 or 40 hands and a box factory and saw mill in Tyngsboro employs about 20.

### TEWKSBURY.

The little village of Phoenix lies close to the Lowell line in the town of Tewksbury. Its sole industry is the Atherton Machine Company, which manufactures cotton openers, spinning frames, lappers and other machinery. It employs 225 men.

At Wamesit, two miles from the city in Tewksbury, are the chemical works of of Taylor & Barker. They manufacture chemicals for dying and printing and employ 18 hands.

### WESTFORD.

On the Stonybrook, at Brookside, is the worsted mill of George C. Moore, employing 125 hands and turning out 600,000 pounds of yarn a year.

At Graniteville are the Abbot worsted mills, owned by John W. Abbot, Allan Cameron and Abiel J. Abbot. The firm also owns a mill in Forge Village. It manufactures carpet yarns and employs 400 hands. The volume of business is $2,000,000 a year.

In Graniteville also are the machine works of Charles G. Sargent's Sons, where 70 men are employed in making wool-washers, dryers, etc.

## POST OFFICE.

### THE BUSY SERVICE PERFORMED BY THE GOVERNMENT.

The first account we have of an effort being made to facilitate correspondence with the outside world by means of an established postal system, was as far back as 1824, two years after the incorporation of the Merrimack Manufacturing Company, when the village numbered a thousand inhabitants. It was then called East Chelmsford. Jonathan C. Morrill was the first postmaster. Two years later the town of

Lowell came into existence and Mr. Morrill's new commission as postmaster of the town was signed April 29, 1826, by President Adams.

Willis P. Burbank, a young business man, is the present incumbent. He is an efficient, able, trustworthy official, with a keen appreciation of the needs of commercial and mercantile Lowell in the line of good mail service. That the office has grown in significance is shown in one way by the increase of salary paid the postmaster in 1824, it was $73; in 1891, it is $3300.

The increase in amount of business for each year is not available, but the figures during three administrations, those of 1852, 1887-'8, and 1890, give a comprehensive and satisfying idea of the increase in, and present size of, the volume of mail business.

In 1852, 881,404 letters, drop letters and papers were received or sent through the office. The gross receipts were $16,438.39; expenses, $4675.71; leaving a net income of $11,762.68.

The business of the office for the year ending July 1, 1888, under Postmaster Haggett, was as follows: Sale of stamps, envelopes, etc., $82,428.87; rent of boxes, $2,890.50; expenses, $34,884.06, a net income of $50,463.32 to the postoffice department. The business had quadrupled its profits in thirty-six years. While this increase in the postal business is quite large, in comparison it is merely ordinary with the growth of the next two years. This is perhaps best illustrated by the financial and statistical report of Postmaster W. P. Burbank, for the fiscal year ending March 31, 1891. The number of pieces of mail delivered by carriers was

ONE OF LOWELL'S OLDEST BLOCKS.

4,688,016, or a daily average of 12,848, and this includes only one half of the receipts, no account being kept of the box or general delivery. A schedule of the mail receipts is as follows:

MAIL DELIVERED.

| Registered letters | | | | 5,373 |
|---|---|---|---|---|
| Letters | - | - | - | 2,051,493 |
| Postals | - | - | - | 490,004 |
| Other mail | - | - | - | 2,141,146 |

MAIL COLLECTED.

| Letters | - | - | - | 1,686,161 |
|---|---|---|---|---|
| Postals | - | - | - | 277,057 |
| Other Mail | - | - | - | 116,743 |

The business of the money order department amounted to $153,326.89; and there were 30,697 registered packages and letters handled.

Other statistics are these: Stamps, postal cards and envelopes sold, $108,-171.22; box rents, $3038.50; total receipts, $111,209.72. Expenditures, employees salaries in postoffice, $13,956.25; rent, $3000; light, $400; compensation to delivery messengers, $570.72; salaries, letter carriers, $21,517.63; miscellaneous expenses, $213.37; incidental expenses, free delivery, $690.20; total, $40,378.17. Deposited with sub-treasurer at Boston, being amount of profit on business, $65,-

681.88; railway P. O. checks paid, $4149.61; total, $111,209.72.

The increase of business brought the office into the first class, numbering 123 offices in the country.

The local service is in the hands of 25 regular letter carriers, four substitute carriers and 17 office clerks. The force is hardly adequate for the business done. To make especially efficient the collecting service a mail wagon for the exclusive purpose of collecting mail is kept. The number of street letter boxes is 155, judiciously distributed. Of this number 50 are on a special circuit with four collections a day, the collections so timed to connect with all the principal out-going mails.

The figures of the above enormous business naturally suggest a good railroad mail service in connection with the efficiency of the local department, and so it is. Lowell is well located as regards railroad lines, being in direct communication with Boston, the North, East and West. There are nine mails to Boston which have direct connection with the New York City, Albany and the western through mails, one leaving as early as 5.10 a. m. A morning and afternoon mail with closed pouch connects with the trans-continental express which leaves Vanceborough, Me., and is scheduled through to Tampa, Fla., Los Angeles and San Francisco, Cal., also other mails connecting with limited expresses for the South and Southwest. There are six mails daily for Portland and points East.

Lowell's postal service is very good and when the new postoffice is erected, the business will have ample room to expand.

## MUNICIPAL.

### THE CITY GOVERNMENT, ITS PERSONNEL AND EXPENDITURES.

The City Council appropriated for the running expenses of the government this year, $918,200.00. The following amounts are important as showing the liberal manner in which provision is made for the several departments:

| | |
|---|---|
| Schools | $160,000.00 |
| School houses | 25,000.00 |
| Roads and bridges | 75,000.00 |
| Police | 70,000.00 |
| Fire department | 80,000.00 |
| Sewers and drains | 20,000.00 |
| Parks | 8,000.00 |
| Lighting | 55,000.00 |
| Library | 12,000.00 |
| Health | 25,000.00 |

In addition to these appropriations loans have been sanctioned for the construction of a new High School building.

The City Council consists of a mayor, a board of seven aldermen, elected at large, a common council of 24 members, elected by wards, four for each of the six wards in the city.

The following is the City Council for 1891:

MAYOR,
GEORGE W. FIFIELD.

ALDERMEN,
Jeremiah Crowley Chairman.
Richard B. Allen,
James W. Cassidy,
Jeremiah Crowley,
Watson A. Dickinson,
Thomas J. Enwright,
George II. Frye,
Stephen B. Puffer.
George F. Tilton.

COMMON COUNCIL,
Thomas J. Sparks—President.

WARD ONE.
Patrick H. Barry,
James F. Doherty,
Peter F. Garrity,
John J. Sullivan.

WARD TWO.
Newell Abare,
Adolph Benard,
Walter C. Coburn,
George H. Marston.

WARD THREE.
Patrick J. Baxter,
John J. Gilbride,
Charles L. Marren,
Thomas J. Sparks.

WARD FOUR.
Edwin L. Giles,
Fred Horne,
Wallace E. Parkin,
Eugene C. Wallace.

WARD FIVE.
Herbert M. Jacobs.
George D. Kimball,
James A. Speirs,
Louis P. Turcotte.

WARD SIX.
James A. Cawley,
James J. Dolan,
Daniel D. Driscoll,
James Gookin.

The government of the city is operated through several departments which are under the direct control of the Board of Aldermen and the City Council. They are:

The Department of Police, Charles Howard, chief.

The Department of Fire, Edward S. Hosmer, chief.

The Department of Streets and Sewers, Horace P. Beals, superintendent.

The Department of Public Buildings, Patrick Bray, superintendent.

The Department of Engineering, George Bowers, chief engineer.

44

City clerk, Michael J. Dowd.
City treasurer, Austin K. Chadwick.
City auditor, David Chase.
City messenger, Henry Hoole.

The schools of the city are under the control of a School Board elected by wards.

The School Board of 1891 is as follows:

CHAIRMAN,
GEORGE W. FIFIELD.

VICE CHAIRMAN,
WALTER COBURN.

The Mayor and President of the Common Council Ex-officiis.

| | |
|---|---|
| Lawrence Cummings, | Patrick Keyes, Jr., |
| Greenleaf C. Brock, | William H. Lathrop, |
| George M. Harrigan, | John W. McEvoy, |
| Fred Woodlies, | Ransom A. Greene, |
| Walter Coburn, | Andrew G. Swapp, |
| Leonard Huntress, | Almon W. Hill. |

Superintendent—Arthur K. Whitcomb.

Supervisor of evening schools—John A. Smith.

The department of health is under the Board of Health.

Charles R. Costello, chairman; Dr. James B. Fields, secretary; Dr. William P. Lawler, city physician; F. A. Bates, superintendent; H. H. Knapp, clerk.

The department of the poor is under the jurisdiction of a Board of Overseers of the Poor. The Mayor, ex-officio; Charles F. Varnum, Alfred Leblanc, W. H. I. Hayes, Freeman W. Puffer, E. W. Lovejoy, Jas. S. Hanson. Clerk, James F. Walsh; Secretary, Charles H. Richardson; Superintendent of Poor Farm, Albert Pinder; Superintendent of Reform School, William A. Lang.

The taxes are assessed by a board of three assessors supplemented by six assistant assessors. The principal assessors are Abel Wheeler, chairman; James Scott and Nathan D. Pratt. Clerk, Stephen J. Kirby.

## SCHOOLS.

LOWELL'S LIBERAL PROVISION FOR THE EDUCATION OF HER CHILDREN — FOR
SCHOOLS, $196,587.

There was expended for instruction, supplies, etc., in the Lowell public schools in 1890, $196,587.48. Of this sum, $141,090.78 was paid for instruction in the day schools. The expense of the evening elementary and high schools, was $16,698.25, and the total expense of the evening drawing school was $4,899.45.

The expense of the schoolhouse department was $83,002.93. There was expended $16,079 for the Cabot street school building, $16,715.43 for the Cross street schoolhouse and $14,487.68 for the Highland school annex.

More than eleven thousand children attended the public schools of Lowell last year.

The history of the Lowell public schools properly begins when, in 1826, the first school committee of the town established ten new school districts in addition to the Chelmsford school districts in existence before the incorporation of the new town.

The first school committee consisted of Rev. Theodore Edson, who justly deserves the title of " father and founder of the school system of Lowell "; Warren Colburn, superintendent of the Merrimack Mills; Samuel Batchelder, a many-sided

man of high literary culture, a devotee of science, and, above all, of the highest inventive genius; Dr. John O. Green, who by his constant visits to the schools showed his devoted interest to the cause of education, and Dr. Elisha Huntington, a graduate of Dartmouth College, a man of high social and literary culture.

The town of Lowell continued the district system of schools from its incorporation, in 1826, to 1832, when the graded system now in vogue was adopted. In that year the school board voted to establish two large graded schools after the manner of the graded schools of Boston and Newburyport. To accomplish this object required the erection of two large schoolhouses at an expense of $20,000.

In the town meeting held to consider that most important subject, Rev. Dr. Edson, single-handed, advocated the expenditure and won by eleven majority. A second town meeting was called to rescind the vote if possible, and Lawrence & Robinson, eminent attorneys, appeared for the opposition. The independent vote had time to do something between the two meetings and the majority in favor of the change was increased to 38. The buildings now known as the Edson and Bartlett schools were then erected.

February 23, 1833, the pupils first occupied the building now known as the Edson school-house. It was first known as the South Grammar school, then as the First Grammar school and finally as the Edson school. The latter name is most appropriate, as the school is one of the two graded schools for which Rev. Dr. Edson so persistently fought.

Joshua Merrill, who began to teach Nov. 5, 1827, was the first teacher in the Edson school, and the principals subsequently were Perley Balch, Ira Waldron and Calvin W. Burbank.

The Bartlett school received its name from Dr. Elisha Bartlett, the first mayor of Lowell. Its present principal is Samuel Bement.

The Green school was first opened in a brick building in Middle street, and when larger accommodations were needed in 1871 the present elegant building in Merrimack street was erected at a cost of $106,-000. The school is named in honor of Dr. John O. Green, one of the members of the first school committee. A. L. Bacheller has been principal since 1880.

The Moody grammar school, established in 1841, was named in honor of Paul Moody, one of the pioneers in the great manufacturing industries. On a petition signed by Gen. Butler and other citizens, the school committee recommended nearly ten years ago the erection of a more modern building for school purposes in a more central location of Belvidere. The city council of this year took up the matter and are to erect a handsome school building on Rogers and High streets.

William S. Greene is the present principal of the Moody school.

The Colburn school-house was erected in 1848, and at the dedication Dec. 13th of that year, Rev. Dr. Edson delivered an address of great historical value. George W. Howe was appointed principal in 1880.

The Varnum school-house is erected near the site of the "Dracut Academy," and was named in honor of Major-Gen. Joseph B. Varnum. The school was opened in 1851 in the upper room of the old academy building and the present edifice was first occupied in 1857. D. P. Galloupe was principal of this school for 25 years and he was succeeded by Arthur K. Whitcomb, the present superintendent.

The Franklin school-house was erected in 1840, and was used for grammar-school purposes until Jan. 1, 1882, when the Highland school-house was erected. People who did not have confidence enough in the future growth of Lowell looked upon the building as unnecessary. It was only a few years when it was again found necessary to use a portion of the Franklin school building for grammar school pupils. Subsequently a four-room addition was made to the Highland school building to accommodate the pupils. Charles W. Morey is the principal of the school.

The Mann school building was erected in 1838 for grammar school purposes and continued to be used as a day school until September, 1884, when Oliver C. Semple was transferred to the principalship of the Pawtucketville grammar school. During the winter months the Mann school is used for the free evening drawing school. The school building was named in honor of Hon. Horace Mann, the distinguished secretary of the state board of education.

The Butler school, named in honor of Lowell's distinguished citizen, was erected in 1883, at an expense of about $56,000. The first principal was George E. Conley, afterward superintendent of the Lowell schools and now a member of the Boston board of supervisors of instruction. His successor as principal was Cornelius F. Callahan, the present incumbent. Owing to the increase in population there is not room enough in the Butler school building. In addition to the eight recitation rooms there are two classes in the school hall and one grammar school room in the Weed street primary school-house. The school committee has recommended two propositions to the city council to overcome the crowded condition of school buildings in that section. The first is to erect a four-room addition to the Butler school-house, and the second is to erect a brick building on land owned by the city in Chelmsford street. It is intended if the latter proposition is accepted to have a portion of the building devoted to grammar school pupils and the remainder to primaries.

The Pawtucket school was erected in 1884 at an expense of nearly $53,000. It is the only grammar school house in Lowell which bears the Indian name of its location. The principals have been Oliver C. Semple, Cyrus W. Irish, Miss Nellie McDonald and William P. Barry.

Brief mention only can be made of the

Washington, Adams and Hancock schools, which have ceased to exist.

During the past five years a number of new buildings, devoted to the primary school children, have been erected at the request of the school committee. They include the buildings in Church, Favor, Charles, Cross and Cabot streets.

For years the school committee has requested that a new high school building be erected at or near the present location and the committees of the city council have the matter under consideration.

Our high school was first opened in December, 1831, under the principalship of Thomas M. Clarke, now Episcopal bishop of Rhode Island, in a small building on Middlesex and Elliott streets.

C. C. Chase, who was principal of the school for years, says for a long time the high school lived a very nomadic life. It was first in the lower room of what is now the Free Chapel in Middlesex street; next in the upper room in the present Edson school house; next in the Concert hall, which was near the site of the present store of A. G. Pollard & Co., in Merrimack street; next in the present Bartlett school house; next in the attic of St. Mary's church in Suffolk street, and next for a second time in the Free chapel. In 1840 it was located in Kirk and Anne streets. Owing to the crowded condition of the building some of the pupils are obliged to attend sessions in the annex in the Worthen street school building.

In the school report for 1890 Supt. Lawton says the average number of pupils belonging to the high school was 474 and the amount paid for teaching in that school was $13,779.15.

From 1840 to 1867 the sexes were separated in the high school and the principals of the female department were Lucy E. Penhallow, Susan E. Burdick and Annie B. Sawyer.

In referring to this school it is a pleasure to every citizen to mention the long and faithful services of C. C. Chase and James S. Russell, who are still residents of Lowell.

The present principal is Frank F. Coburn, who succeeded Mr. Chase in 1883.

### EVENING SCHOOLS.

Previous to 1855 free evening schools were maintained in Lowell by the Lowell Missionary association. It was decided in 1855 to bring the schools under the supervision of the school committee. After John A. Smith was elected a member of the school committee in 1880 he gave evening schools his special attention. When the day school rooms were freely opened for evening school pupils the attendance rapidly increased. In 1885 Mr. Smith was elected supervisor of evening schools. During the session which closed March 1st of this year, the High, Green, Bartlett, Moody, Colburn, Butler, Franklin, Varnum and the new school building in Aiken avenue were opened for the attendance of evening school pupils.

### FREE EVENING DRAWING SCHOOLS.

Three evening classes in drawing were formed in 1872, one in free hand, one in architectural and one in machine drawing. The sessions were held for some time in the Green school hall, afterward in the Worthen street school house. This free institution has continued with gratifying success and with increasing favor.

### PRIVATE SCHOOLS.

There are eleven private schools in Lowell. These include the parochial schools which have been established under the auspices of four of the Catholic churches.

There are three schools connected with St. Patrick's church. The female academy, which was established in 1852; second, the parochial school for girls. Both schools are under the direction of the Sisters of Notre Dame.

St. Patrick's school for boys is under charge of the Xaverian Brothers.

The parochial school of the Immaculate Conception church was opened in 1881 and is under the instruction of the Grey Nuns of Ottawa. The school is for both sexes.

St. Joseph's parochial school in Moody street is designed for the children of French Catholics. The pupils are under the instruction of the Grey Nuns of Ottawa. Recently, Rev. Andrew Garin of the Oblate Order purchased land and buildings in Merrimack street, nearly opposite the church of St. Jean de Baptiste. It is intended to have a parochial school for boys, which will be placed in charge of an order

TALBOT BUILDING, MIDDLE STREET.

yet to be selected by the pastor with the consent of the archbishop.

St. Michael's parochial school in Sixth street in Centralville is in charge of the Dominican Sisters. The pupils are all girls. As in the other parochial schools it is under the supervision of the pastor.

The number of pupils attending private schools in Lowell is estimated to be over 4000.

#### TRAINING SCHOOL.

A training school has recently been established by the school committee for the instruction of candidates for positions as teachers. The principal and her assistants are to report to the committee on teachers and training school as to the aptness and ability of the candidates. Pupil-teachers who fail to receive the required rank can be re-admitted for another trial by a majority vote of the committee on teachers and training school. Since the establishment of this school all teachers assigned positions have been graduates of the training school.

#### SUPERINTENDENTS OF SCHOOLS.

In 1859 George W. Shattuck was elected superintendent of schools, but the citizens, at the following municipal election, decided that they did not want any superintendent.

In February, 1864, the subject was again discussed, and Abner J. Phipps of New Bedford consented to accept the position when the late Hon. Hocum Hosford, then mayor, agreed to pay the salary if the city council declined to do so. He served until the close of 1866, when he tendered his resignation. His successors have been Charles Morrill, who died in 1884, George E. Conley, who was afterwards elected one of the supervisors of the Boston public schools, George F. Lawton, formerly principal of the Green school and Arthur K. Whitcomb, the present incumbent.

#### CARNEY MEDALS.

At the graduation exercises of the high school each year six silver medals are presented to the scholars in the school, three for boys and three for girls. These medals are the result of the gift of James G. Carney, first treasurer of the Lowell Institution for Savings. The distribution began in 1859, and at the head of the list is the name of Frederick T. Greenhalge, whose term as representative in Congress from this district expired March 4th of this year.

#### SCHOOL COMMITTEE.

The school committee includes the mayor and president of the common council and two members chosen for terms of two years each for the six wards of the city.

## FIRE DEPARTMENT.

THE CITY'S CONCERN FOR THE SAFETY OF PUBLIC AND PRIVATE PROPERTY —FOR FIRE DEPARTMENT $99,928.

Lowell luck, as touching its continued immunity from extensive loss by fire, is proverbial throughout the state. It is not, however, upon that good fortune alone that Lowell depends for its excellent reputation as touching the safety of its property from extensive fires.

To begin with, the city of Lowell possesses many natural advantages whose presence in the long run cannot but make themselves felt in the small total loss which is suffered annually. With but trifling exceptions, and with all those exceptions occurring in the safest districts in the city from a fireman's point of view, Lowell has been built upon level ground, a fact that means the gain of valuable minutes in

the prompt response of its fire department to an alarm in any part of the city.

In addition to this advantage, the city has, when all its elements are taken into consideration, a water service that will compare only to its own advantage with that of any city in New England. What with its abundant and never failing city service and the almost innumerable canals in the district upon which the city stands, the city presents at every point of its wide extent a supply of water for fire-lighting that is not only inexhaustible but readily available at any point. This abundance of water and the ease with which it can be handled, has enabled every corporation and manufacturing industry to introduce and maintain at its own expense its own private fire service.

In view of these advantages, the city of Lowell is enabled to guarantee excellent protection from fire to her industries and her residents with what, regarded simply in a numerical sense, will pass as a small fire department. That the size of a fire department is, however, of secondary importance as compared with its system and activity, is plainly evident in the table of losses which Lowell has to present.

The active fire department of Lowell is made up of four steam fire engines, including a new and large machine which has been recently added.

Around the Central Fire Station in which this machine stands at the very heart of the city, the other machines have been stationed so as to be as nearly equidistant in their directions, as possible. In the handling of its heavier apparatus, the department has recently introduced the three-horse hitch with excellent results in the matter of running time.

In addition to the steam fire engines and their full equipments, the department comprises five hose companies whose houses are so disposed to form a larger circle outside that in which the steam engines are located. The most recent improvement in this part of the fire service has been the disbanding of the old hand-line companies and the replacing of them by house companies with all the latest equipments.

The department also has three hook and ladder companies, whose equipment includes a heavy Babcock truck and extension ladder; two chemical engines and a protective wagon which responds to all alarms and is provided with a full equipment of extinguishers, folding ladders, covers, a Spencer canvas chute and a Dixon arrow gun. The work of this company since its introduction into the department has been remarkable for its effective promptness in response to alarms, and for the extent to which its efforts have prevented damage by water in small or badly located fires.

The steamers of the department are manned by companies of twelve, five of whom are permanent firemen. The hose companies are composed of nine men

each, three of whom are permanent. The hook and ladder companies have three, five and eight permanent men. respectively, with full companies of ten, twelve and thirteen members. The protective company is made up of five permanent men. The apparatus of the department is well housed, being, with the single exception of the hose carriage house in Ayer City, provided with substantial brick buildings for the most part new, and in all cases fitted with the latest improvements for the work of the department. The Central Fire Station erected at a cost of nearly $65,000 is justly regarded as a model of its kind, in the possession of which the city may well take a pardonable pride.

The fire alarm telegraph service consists of eighty signal boxes with their ninety miles or more of wires, all of which is under the care of an electrician as the head of this sub-department. The Gamewell signal service, which has also been recently introduced in the police department, is capable of employment in the fire alarm service.

The record of losses by fire which Lowell has sustained during the last twenty years is indeed an excellent one, and one which signifies vastly more than a mere continuance of good fortune.

The cost of this department for the year 1890, was but a few dollars in excess of that of the police department, being $99,928.19.

The head of this department is Chief Edward S. Hosmer, a fireman who has learned his trade not from books or stories of other men's work, but from an experience of thirty-two years of service in the department of which he is now the head. Mr. Hosmer was born in Lowell, in 1838, and first joined the department in May, 1856. From that time until the present, with the exception of a period of three years, he has been in continuous service in the department. He was made assistant engineer in 1872, and was first appointed chief of the department in 1885, holding that position for two terms of one year each. Mr. Hosmer was again appointed chief of the department in 1888, the term of office having been changed from one to three years.

# POLICE.

A WELL EQUIPPED AND THOROUGHLY ORGANIZED DEPARTMENT—FOR POLICE $99,839.

The organization of the police department upon its present basis came necessarily and naturally with the incorporation of Lowell as a city, in May, 1836. The city employs a large and well-disciplined force which performs its work with the aid of more than a fair share of the equipments and conveniences of modern suggestion. The headquarters of the police department, together with its court, a city dispensary and the offices of one or two minor city officials are located in the Market Building on Market street, one hundred yards from Central at the very heart of the city. A part of this building was formerly used as an armory and the rooms vacated by the military companies have been utilized to provide recreative and sleeping accommodations for the members of the force.

In its present form the police department is made up of a chief and two deputies, four inspectors, three sergeants, three warrant and court officers, two keepers, fifteen day patrolmen and forty-four night patrolmen. In addition to these are one officer detailed for special duty, two drivers, five supernumerary officers and a police matron ; eighty-three persons in all. The department is conducted in accordance with the regulations of the civil service, and the force is made up in a large degree of young and active officers reduced to a fine state of discipline and efficiency under the guidance of the higher police officials who have made police work a life-long study.

As a general characteristic the administration of the police department of Lowell is energetic and at the same time governed by a wholesome conservatism that rarely allows and never countenances any course of action which places the department in a false light.

Among its other good qualities the department is possessed of a remarkably successful detective force, the services of which is of such a nature as to inspire a

wholesome fear in the minds of such evildoers as may come within its jurisdiction.

During the last police year, ending Nov. 30, 1890, the efficiency of the department has been greatly increased by the introduction of the Gamewell Police Telephone and Signal System, consisting in its present extent, of fifty-three street signal boxes and a four circuit central office plant. In addition to this system the department has been provided with a stable adjoining the station where the horses of the patrol wagon are kept. The signal system has already proved of great service to the department, and with the extension of which it is capable, it will serve to put off the time when an extension of the district to be patrolled and a growth of the population will necessitate the division of the city into districts each with its separate station house.

The police department, as shown by its record for the past year, has never been at a higher point of discipline and efficiency than at present. This department cost the city in the year from December 1, '89, to November 30, '90, the sum of $99,839.32.

Chief of Police Charles Howard, appointed to his first term in that capacity on Jan. 6th of the current year, is probably one of the most widely known police officials in the state. Mr. Howard was born in Lowell in 1842 and entered the service of the department in 1871. He was appointed sergeant in 1881 and promoted to the rank of captain Jan. 9, 1882. In this capacity he served until March, 1890, when he was appointed deputy chief.

Chief Howard has ever shown himself an energetic and conscientious officer in the discharge of the duties of the various positions in the service which he has been called upon to fill, and his appointment to the highest office of the department which he has so long and so faithfully served is regarded with complete satisfaction by both political parties.

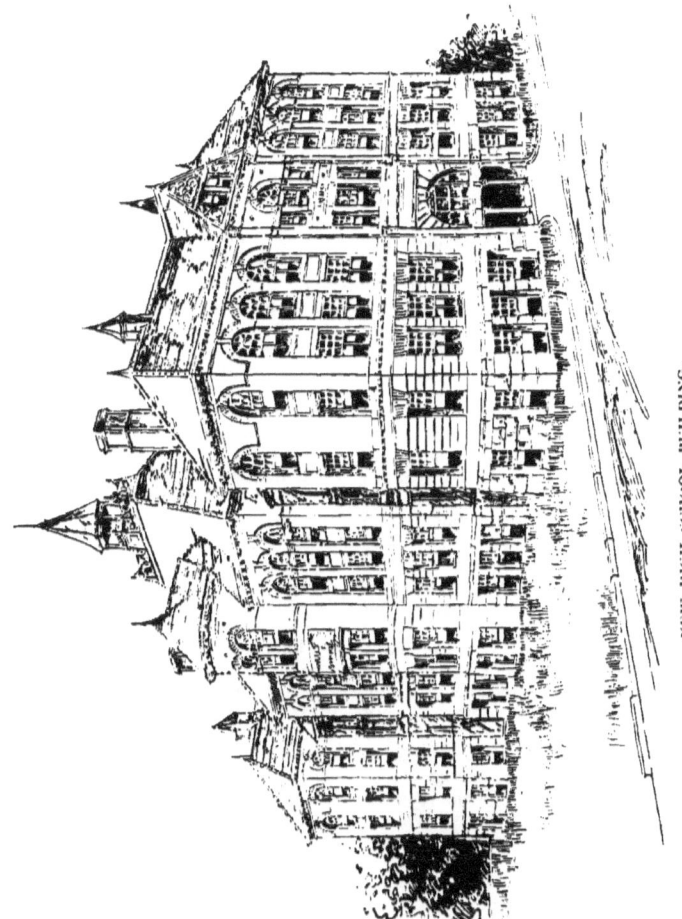

NEW HIGH SCHOOL BUILDING.

# WATER WORKS.

## THE MOST COMPLETE SYSTEM IN NEW ENGLAND.

The public water service of Lowell is one of the most important of the municipal institutions. Up to the time of the introduction of the present system of water supply for the city, it had depended upon a supply furnished from the Locks and Canals Company, and from other private sources.

The life of the present system dates from an act of the legislature of the year 1855. Under this act and an additional act of the year 1866, giving additional power together with the minor acts of later date, the present system of water works was constructed. The board of water commissioners was elected and organized January 28, 1870, and the construction of the water works occupied about three years under the supervision of this board.

The plan which was finally adopted as the best, when all things were taken into consideration, consisted of a supply from the Merrimack River.

From the intake situated 1500 feet above the Pawtucket dam, the water is conducted to the terminal chamber and thence to the pumping station, which is located on land in Centralville.

The pumping plant comprises at present two powerful engines, one of which has not only an interesting history, but a proud record in actual service, as well.

In 1872, Henry J. Morris of Philadelphia built an engine for the Spring Garden water works of that city, which attracted the attention of the Lowell engineers on account of the results obtained from a small expenditure of coal. This engine was guaranteed to raise 75,000,000 lbs. of water one foot on 100 lbs. of coal, but in the tests made far exceeded that strength. The guaranteed capacity of such an engine was five millions of gallons per day while the daily average consumption of Lowell at that time was only about 500,000 gallons.

Opinions differed as to the advisability of ordering so powerful a machine: but in the end the wiser opinion of the engineers prevailed and an order was given for the construction of a similar engine. The original Morris engine was the first high duty engine of any importance that had been constructed in this country; but the Lowell machine was made its undoubted superior by important changes in its valve gear at the suggestion of one of the Lowell engineers.

Mr. Morris built the engine at a cost of $75,000 to the city of Lowell, and lost $20,000 by the operation. Shortly after its completion, in the year 1873, the Morris works were burned and the patterns were destroyed. The Spring Garden engine after which the Lowell engine was built, has long ago been broken up, leaving the Lowell engine the only one of its kind in existence.

As totally unlike this engine as it is possible, and still be a pumping engine, is the Worthington engine which stands by its side. The Worthington is a horizontal engine of the same guaranteed capacity as its big neighbor, and was set up as a relief engine in 1877. Its cost was only $36,000.

The increase in the amount of water consumed each day since the Morris engine was built has been enormous. In 1873, the daily average consumption was 511,474 gallons; in 1876, when the Worthington was introduced it had risen to 1,488,950 gallons; while at the present time it exceeds five and one quarter millions of gallons. Nine millions of gallons have been drawn from the reservoir in a single period of twenty-four hours.

In accordance with a warning derived from two instances, in which both engines have been temporarily incapacitated for duty and in obedience to a continually increasing demand upon the water supply, the city has recently awarded contracts for a second Worthington engine of 12,-000,000 gallons capacity, the setting up of which will necessitate an extensive enlargement of the pumping station.

The water works comprises two enormous reservoirs located in the highlands of Centralville. The reservoir first built and which has proven itself of sufficient capacity and elevation to supply the whole city, except certain portions of Centralville and Belvidere, is situated on the east side of Beacon street, at the head of Sixth. The reservoir basin is in itself five hundred and twenty feet long, five hundred and ten feet wide and twenty-four feet deep at high water mark, which is four feet below the top of the embankment. This reservoir contains, at high water mark, 30,000,000 gallons, or enough to supply the city for a week at its present rate of consumption. The reservoir has a large relative elevation to the main level of the city and an absolute elevation of 181.5 feet.

In addition to this source of the city's supply, a second, or high service reservoir, was constructed in 1881 on the hill above the general reservoir. The capacity of the high service reservoir is 1,500,000 gallons and its elevation 253.5 feet.

From the latest figures available, the city water works earn in round numbers $200,000 per year. Its mains extend to a total length of about 92 miles, and its number of services is nearly 10,000. It maintains 850 hydrants in the fire service and has an annual pay roll of $33,000. It has always been the policy of the board by which the water works are controlled, to extend its mains readily in obedience to the demands made upon the service. The gross cost of the water works to Jan. 1, 1891, were $4,841,227.27, and the receipts to the same date $2,453,398.47, leaving the net cost of works at that date, $2,387,828.80.

The following table will show, exclusive of interest on the debt, the general success of the water works supply from a business point of view for the past eighteen years:

| | Expenditures. | Receipts. | Expenditures in excess of receipts. | Receipts in excess of expenditures. |
|---|---|---|---|---|
| 1873 | $188,376.59 | $ 57,739.48 | $130,637.11 | |
| 1874 | 128,105.63 | 80,625,65 | 47,179.98 | |
| 1875 | 170,095.78 | 94,968.44 | 75,187.64 | |
| 1876 | 115,012.21 | 98,815.51 | 16,196.70 | |
| 1877 | 53,988.72 | 100,826.63 | | $ 46,837.91 |
| 1878 | 49,900.15 | 104,142.87 | | 54,242.72 |
| 1879 | 42,157.82 | 110,185.34 | | 68,027.52 |
| 1880 | 45,031.59 | 123,710.49 | | 78,708.90 |
| 1881 | 121,601.27 | 128,053.97 | | 6,452.70 |
| 1882 | 64,025.92 | 110,897.96 | | 75,872.04 |
| 1883 | 65,673.23 | 152,582.99 | | 86,909.76 |
| 1884 | 64,062.71 | 154,437.55 | | 80,434.84 |
| 1885 | 64,030.21 | 157,956.79 | | 93,926.55 |
| 1886 | 51,808.52 | 168,757.53 | | 116,919.01 |
| 1887 | 62,236.05 | 178,234.29 | | 115,998.24 |
| 1888 | 75,234.73 | 183,127.37 | | 107,892.64 |
| 1889 | 80,554.68 | 189,247.66 | | 108,692.98 |
| 1890 | 78,073.46 | 193,963.80 | | 115,890.31 |

The bonded debt of the water works was in a large part refunded at a low rate of interest on the maturity of its first bonds in November, 1890. The refunding will reduce materially the annual expenditures on account of the works.

The water works are controlled, in accordance with an amended ordinance of 1888, by a water board of five members, to be elected each year, by concurrent vote of the City Council, one from the Board of Aldermen and four others, who shall be citizens holding no other municipal office, one being chosen each year for a term of four years.

The water rate per family—and that includes water closet, bath, hose and water for horse and cow — is $23 a year, an exceptionally low figure.

## THE CITY LIBRARY.

AN INSTITUTION WHICH ENLIGHTENS THE PUBLIC AT THE PUBLIC EXPENSE—FOR THE LIBRARY $14,500.

What is now known and appreciated as the City Library of Lowell, had its beginning in the City School Library which came into existence under an ordinance of the City Council, passed May 20, 1844.

The City Library of Lowell is one of the few institutions of its kind which owes its origin solely to municipal action.

Established at first in pursuance of certain resolves of the state legislature, authorizing cities and towns to establish and maintain school libraries, this institution has, from the opening of its doors on February 11, 1845, occupied a much wider field of usefulness than that which was comprehended in the idea which led to its foundation. In the year 1860, this feature of its existence had become so widely recognized that an ordinance was passed changing the name to that of City Library, which, in the process of incorporation, became changed to the present legal title of the institution, City Library of Lowell.

After one previous attempt in 1878, a nominal annual fee of fifty cents for the privileges of the library was abolished in 1883, and it thus became an absolutely free institution. In the same year the library established its first free reading room which was followed five years later by the establishment of a special free reading room for women. Both of these adjuncts to the work of the library have been uniformly successful in affording the best of facilities to the large numbers of both sexes who have availed themselves of the privileges thus placed within their reach.

With the accession of Mayor Palmer in 1888, came the final act which made the City Library thoroughly an institution of the people and removed from it the last trace of the influence of political management and interference. An act of the legislature passed in that year incorporated a board of trustees for the library, composed of the Mayor, ex-officio, and five

MEMORIAL BUILDING.
To be used as a
PUBLIC LIBRARY.

Frederick W. Studley
Architect, Lowell, Mass.

other citizens by him appointed with the approval of the Board of Aldermen. To these trustees, each holding office for five years, one retiring annually, was committed the entire management of the affairs of the library.

In proportion to the development of its advantages, the library has continued to grow in size and usefulness under the guidance of wise selections from among Lowell's most prominent citizens to be its trustees, until the recent reverse inflicted upon it by the damage from fire to its quarters, found it with 45,000 well-selected volumes upon its shelves, including a carefully selected reference library, and an annual circulation of about 115,000 volumes.

For several years, the city of Lowell has recognized the pressing need of more commodious accommodations for this most useful of all its public institutions, and no plan for the utilization of the city hall lot has been considered complete until it should present ample provisions for that need.

The building which is now being erected with the double purpose of commemorating Lowell's dead soldiers and furnishing ample quarters for the City Library will compare favorably in appearance and appointments with the other library buildings of the state.

The occupation of this new building, which will not long be delayed, will add a new and important element to the usefulness and accessibility of the City Library.

The appropriation for the City Library for 1889 was $14,500, and the total expenditures $18,191.44, of which sum $6500 in round numbers was devoted to the purchase and binding of new volumes. The Library adds annually about 3000 volumes to its number.

The trustees of the Library at this time are Mayor Fifield, Hon. George F. Richardson, Frank P. Putnam, Thomas Walsh, Larkin T. Trull and Dr. Stephen T. Johnson.

## MILITARY.

### LOWELL'S MARTIAL RECORD AND PRESENT FORCE.

A bright page in Lowell's history is that upon which are inscribed the deeds of valor of her citizen soldiery. The records are without a parallel from one end of the continent to the other; the city is justly famed for the part she has taken and the position maintained in the many struggles since her founding.

Her military history opens many years ago when New England was a wilderness over which roamed the redskin. For mutual protection, the settlers on the banks of the Merrimack organized into armed bodies, and as early as 1656, a major-general, one Daniel Gookin, assumed military jurisdiction over the region round about Pawtucket Falls. The settlers took an active part against hostile Indians during King Phillip's war, and in 1688, under Major Henchman, fought many battles on the banks of the river. From this time forward, there was always an armed force in the settlement, then Chelmsford, now Lowell. To the French and Indian war was contributed a company of men, which constituted a part of the attacking force on the Louisburg fortress. The first step taken, however, and which has proven the foundation of Lowell's later military history, was the part taken by the soldiers of Chelmsford at the battle of Bunker Hill, and through subsequent events of the Revolution. It was not until September, 1859, that the services of these soldiers were fittingly recognized when a monument to their bravery and patriotism was dedicated in Chelmsford. The town was also represented in the struggle of 1812, and among the famous warriors was Commodore Perry, the hero of Putin Bay, whose descendants are still resident in Lowell.

The first militia company organized after Lowell came into existence was the Mechanics' Phalanx, on July 4th, 1825, which company has the past winter celebrated its sixty-sixth birthday. Numerous companies sprang up during subsequent years, but only a few became permanent. Among the former were the Highlanders in 1841, who carried pikes, the City Guard in 1841, the Watson Light Guard in 1851, and the Lawrence Cadets in 1855. Many of Lowell's foremost men served in the militia during the early days, notably Gen. B. F. Butler, who joined the City Guards as a private and rose step by step to the position of brigadier-general of volunteer militia before the war. It is in the Civil war that Lowell shines conspicuous, for she was the first to respond with men and money for the defence of the Union, and she gave the first martyrs to the cause.

The fall of Sumter produced a sensation in the city of spindles and President Lincoln's call for troops found an immediate response from the troops in Lowell, consisting of four companies, Co. C, Mechanics' Phalanx, Capt. Follansbee; Co. D, City Guards, Capt. J. W. Hart; Co. H, Watson Guards, Capt. J. F. Noyes;

Co. A, Lawrence Cadets, afterwards National Greys, Capt. Sawtelle. These four companies were mustered April 16th, 1861, and joined the Sixth Regiment in Boston the next morning. The regiment was then ordered to the defence of the National Capitol, and on the 19th Baltimore was reached. Two Lowell companies started to cross the city and while doing so were attacked by an infuriated mob, and there, on Pratt street, was shed the first blood of the war, Addison O. Whitney, Luther C. Ladd and Charles A. Taylor of the City Guards being the martyrs. The remains of Ladd and Whitney were brought to Lowell on May 6th, 1861, and buried in the Lowell cemetery, until four years later when they were reinterred under a granite shaft in Monument Square with appropriate and impressive ceremonies.

The Sixth regiment was brigaded under Gen. Butler. Among the other military companies going to the front were the Hill Cadets, afterwards D Co., 16th Battery; Richardson Light Infantry, afterwards Seventh Battery; Abbott Greys, attached to the Second Infantry: G Co., Sixteenth Infantry; Twenty-Sixth Regiment, which was attached to the Department of the Gulf; the Sixth and Seventh batteries early in 1862; the Thirty-First

LOWELL ARMORY.

Infantry at the second call of President Lincoln; and another Sixth Regiment for nine months service which participated in the Suffolk Campaign. In Lowell was also organized the first Soldiers' Aid Association, afterwards the Sanitary Commission.

Lowell's roll of honor was a long one, as hundreds of her citizen soldiers yielded up their lives in defence of the Union. After the war military enthusiasm naturally waned, but the glorious records of past years kept interest centered in the Phalanx and Putnam Guards.

An unfortunate occurrence from a historical stand-point, was the destruction of all records by a fire in 1860 in the Market Street Armory, and afterward another fire in 1869 at the same place.

The companies were afterward moved to a new armory on Middle Street which they occupied for nearly a score years, until fire was again the nemesis of the militia, destroying the building on the night of Jan. 10th, 1888. During the year previous to this, the young blood of the city had become stirred again and D Co., Second Corp of Cadets, of which three other companies belong in Salem, M Co., Ninth Regiment, and the Ambulance Corps connected with the First Brigade Staff were organized and mustered into service. All the organizations flourished despite the fact that they were sadly inconvenienced for proper accommodations.

Now the militia is comfortably quartered in an armory on Westford street, completed and formally opened Dec. 10th, 1890. While perhaps not the largest, it is among the largest, best constructed and most commodious armories in the state.

During the spring of 1888 the urgent need of proper quarters for the companies was brought to the attention of the state legislature and an appropriation of $105,-000 was made. The site selected contained 18,491 square feet. The contracts amounted to $71,089 and eighteen months were required to build the armory. It is a castellated structure, three stories in height, turreted battlements with octagon and round towers and a fine porte cochere entrance. The mean depth including drill shed is 104 feet with an 84-foot front. Interiorly the building is admirably adapted for military purposes. There is a wide vestibule with corridors leading to the doors of company rooms. Each organization has reception, non-commissioned and commissioned officers' rooms, uniform and gun rooms fitted with every convenience. On the first floor are quartered C Co., 6th Regiment and M Co., 9th Regiment; on the second floor, G Co., 6th Regiment and D Co., Second Corps of Cadets; on the third floor, Ambulance Corps, First Brigade. The upper floor is used in part by the regimental drum corps, the gymnasium and the janitor. There is also on the second floor a finely furnished reception room; also an armorer's office, rifle range and bath rooms in the building. The quarters are all lavishly furnished by the companies while the state has completed the building interiorly after the same general style of the exterior. The commandant of the armory is Capt. Orestes M. Pratt, commanding the Mechanics' Phalanx, the present senior officer in the city. The commands are officered as follows: C Co., Capt. O. M. Pratt; Lieuts. G. E. Lull and A. D. Prince; G Co., Capt. W. H. Bean; Lieuts. E. B. Carr and W. F. Miles; D Co., Capt. W. H. Hosmer; Lieut. Alex. Greig; M Co., Capt. C. H. Russell; Lieuts. A. D. Mitten and T. Gauley; Ambulance Corps, Lieut. Myles Standish; Sergts. G. W. Conant and H. D. Pickering.

## LOWELL BOARD OF TRADE.

A PLACE WHERE OUR LIVE BUSINESS MEN MEET TO DISCUSS MATTERS OF IMPORTANCE.

In the early part of 1887, a number of our business men began to agitate the question of forming a local Board of Trade. That there was plenty of work for them to do in the line of advancing the interests of the city went without saying, and on the 23rd of May they effected an organization, suitable quarters having been secured in the Hildreth building, and at once began a vigorous growth. From a score or more originators of the plan the membership increased into the hundreds, and with this growth other accommodations were needed, and the present rooms on the top floor of the Central block were taken and appropriately opened. In its career the Board has distinguished itself by taking up and discussing many questions of importance to the city, and it is at present agitating the question of better railroad facilities between Lowell and Boston.

Within the past few months the office of Secretary has been made a permanent one, so that the Board now has a man always working in its interest to secure the settlement of outside industries in the city, and in attending to other important matters which come up from time to time.

The officers of the Board for 1887-8 were: President, Charles H. Coburn;

vice presidents, Charles E. Adams, George A. Marden, Henry M. Thompson; secretary, Chas. W. Eaton; treasurer, G. Winfield Knowlton; directors, A. G. Pollard, E. N. Wood, Amasa Pratt, R. M. Boutwell, C. H. Hobson.

For the year 1889 the officers were: President, Charles H. Coburn; vice-presidents, Charles E. Adams, Francis Jewett, Edward N. Wood; secretary, Chas. W. Eaton; treasurer, G. Winfield Knowlton; directors, Arthur G. Pollard, R. M. Boutwell, Amasa Pratt, Charles H. Hobson, Patrick O'Hearn.

For the year 1890: President, Charles E. Adams; vice-presidents, George A. Marden, Francis Jewett, Edward N. Wood; secretary, Chas. W. Eaton; treasurer, G. Winfield Knowlton; directors, Chas. W. Wilder, Patrick O'Hearn, Prescott C. Gates, Chas. A. Stott, Joseph L. Chalifoux.

The present officers are; President, Chas. E. Adams; vice-presidents, George A. Marden, Francis Jewett, Charles A. Stott; secretary, James T. Smith; treasurer, G. Winfield Knowlton; directors, Joseph L. Chalifoux, Otis A. Merrill, William H. Ward, James O'Sullivan, J. W. C. Pickering.

There is a great and growing field for the Board of Trade, and already its influence is being felt in a profitable manner. The Board is fortunate certainly in securing the valuable services of Mr. Smith.

### LIST OF MEMBERS.

| | |
|---|---|
| Adams, Chas. E. | Hardware, Paints, etc. |
| Allen, Chas. H. | Lumber |
| Abbott, E. T. | Insurance |
| Boutwell, R. M. | Iron and Steel |
| Bateman, A. P. | Lumber |
| Brennan, M. F. | American Bolt Co. |
| Butler, Josiah | Cotton Waste |
| Barnes, Henry W. | Merchant Tailor |
| Bacheller, N. J. N. | Printer |
| Butler, F. H. | Apothecary |
| Burtt, Chas. H. | Carpenter |
| Baker, E. G. | Carpenter |
| Blackburn, A. | Minister of Gospel |
| Bartlett, R. G. | Real Estate |
| Bailey, Frederick | Apothecary |
| Brock, G. C. | Apothecary |
| Bennett, J. W. | Contractor |
| Boutwell, R. H. | Iron and Steel |
| Benner, E. J. | Furniture |
| Bagley, G. W. | Carpenter |
| Batchelder, Geo. W. | Lawyer |
| Burbank, W. P. | Postmaster |
| Burke, John C. | Lawyer |
| Blake, Chas. E. | Master Mechanic |
| Brazer, Wm. P. | Furnishing Goods |
| Butterfield, Edwin G. | Printer |

| | |
|---|---|
| Coburn, C. H. | Paints, Oils. &c. |
| Coggeshall, J. H. | H. R. Barker M'f'g Co. |
| Chalifoux, J. L. | Clothing |
| Collins, Michael | Manufacturer |
| Coburn, Walter | Cotton Waste |
| Cushing, Jos. L. | Galvanized Iron |
| Conant, E. B. | Auctioneer |
| Cheney, C. W. | Fancy Groceries |
| Coburn, E. F. | Paints, Oils, &c. |
| Chase, James A. | Stable Keeper |
| Carter, Chas. E. | Apothecary |
| Church, F. C. | Insurance |
| Connors, P. P. | Coal, Lime, &c. |
| Carney, Geo. J. | Treasurer Savings Bank |
| Crosby, C. T. | Furniture Manufacturer |
| Carolin, Thomas | Real Estate |
| Cluin, John J. | Jeweller |
| Carll, Francis | Real Estate |
| Chamberlain, C. T. | Undertaker |
| Clement, Geo. W. | Lawyer |
| Cumnock, A. G. | Agent B. Cotton Mills |
| Callaghan, John | Stoves, &c. |
| Currier, J. B. | Undertaker |
| Cushing, H. G. | Sheriff |
| Church, H. C. | Insurance |
| Cheney, John L. | Bobbin Manufacturer |
| Corbett, M. | Provisions |
| Coburn, Clarence G. | Grocer |
| Chadwick, A. M. | Paymaster |
| Coburn, Frank | Insurance, &c. |
| Chase, David | City Auditor |
| Conlon, Patrick | Contractor |
| Clarke, Alfred | Electrician |
| Connell, Thos. H. | Contractor |
| Coburn, Geo. B. | Insurance |
| Coughlin, Wm. J. | Real Estate |
| Derbyshire, A. W. | Fancy Groceries |
| Dunlap, Harry | Dry Goods |
| Dexter, S. K. | Commission Merchant |
| Dickinson, W. A. | Soaps, &c. |
| Derby, L. A. | Electrician |
| Dumas, Levi | Bookbinder |
| Dobbins, Richard | Boiler Maker |
| Dempsey, Geo. C. | Clerk |
| David, P. Jr. | Painter |
| Dickey, Charles M. | Hotel Keeper |
| Dudley, D. E. | Life Insurance |
| Donovan, J. J. | Groceries |
| Eaton, Chas. W. | Stock Broker |
| Ela, Horace | Grocer |
| Ellingwood, Edward | Apothecary |
| Entwistle, T. C. | Manufacturer Machinery |
| Elliott, Thomas H. | Real Estate |
| Erskine, C. M. | Grocer |
| Fifield, Geo. W. | Manufacturer Machinery |
| Francis, James | Agent Locks & Canals |
| Fuller, H. C. | Real Estate |
| Flemings, F. J. | Paper |
| Foss, Ether S. | Contractor |
| Foye, W. P. | Grain, &c. |
| Fels, August | Agent M. Woolen Mills |
| French, Josiah B. | Electrician |
| Fox, Fred A. | Farmer |
| Floyd, Warren L. | Architect |
| Fish, Charles T. | Real Estate |
| Ford, F. H. | Architect |
| Gates, Prescott C. | Belting, &c. |
| Glidden, Chas. J. | Treasurer Erie T. C. |
| Gates, R W. | Belting, &c. |
| Gookin, M. F. | Furniture |
| Gould, S. S. | Card Clothing |

Greenhalge, F. T. — Lawyer
Gray, Frank — Provisions
Gray, Albert M. — Provisions
Goodale, F. C. — Apothecary
Gibson, John I. — Apothecary
Greenwood, M. — Grocer
Hobson, Chas. H. — H. R. Barker M'f'g Co.
Harris, A. W. — Paper Hangings, &c.
Harrington, J. H. — Printer
Hanchett, Frank — Commission Merchant
Hanscom, Geo. A. — Printer
Hutchinson, C. C. — Treasurer M. Sav. Bank
Hood, Chas. I. — Patent Medicines
Haworth, John H. — Cop Tube Manufacturer
Holden, Edward D. — Agent Sterling Mills
Huse, Harry V. — Printer
Hylan, E. S. — Manufacturer
Huntoon, Geo. L. — Real Estate
Horne, Frederick — Coal, Wood, &c.
Howe, Henry C. — Lumber
Howe, Frank W. — Lumber
Hosford, A. H. — Carriages
Haggett, A. A. — Paymaster
Houston, A. Clarke — Editor
Howard, John H. — Coal, Wood, &c.
Howe, Chas. E. — Lumber
Hayes, W. H. I. — Cigars, &c.
Huse, Hiram E. — Clothing
Howe, Wm. G. — Carpenter
Hanson, C. H. — Sale Stable
Hanscom, Wm. H. — Printer
Jewett, Francis — Wholesale Provisions
Knowlton, G. W. — Cashier W. Nat'l B'k.
Kittredge, L. F. — Contractor
Kelley, Patrick — Bottler
Kelley, Frank F. — Doors, Sashes, etc.
Kimball, Charles H. — Clothing
Kimball, J. F. — Banker
Knapp, C. L. — Clerk Water Board
Kilgore, J. M. — Life Insurance
Keyes, P. Jr. — Grocer
Littlefield, Chas. — M'f'r Paper Boxes
Littlefield, W. S. — M'f'r Paper Boxes
Livingston, W. E. — Coal, Wood, &c.
Lamson, N. G. — Treas. M. R. Sav. B'k.
Lyon, A. S. — Agent L. M'f'g Co.
Libby, M. V. B. — Blacksmith.
Lyons, E. J. — Janitor.
Lawton, Frederick — Lawyer
Latham, C. H. — M'f'r Wire Goods
Loupret, N. J. — Photographer
Leinhas, W. E. — Furniture
Lee, Thomas C. — Insurance
Lamson, Edwin — Pres. Coburn Shuttle Co
Merrill, Otis A. — Architect
Marden, George A. — Editor
Marston, George H. — Real Estate
Miller, George W. — R. R. Agent
Medina, E. J. — Hair Goods
Manning, George H. — Furniture
Murphy, James — Real Estate
Mitchell, F. G. — Dry Goods, &c.
Merrill, Frank M. — Stationer
Morse, S. Warren — Millinery
Morse, E. H. — Stable Keeper
Mack, W. A. — Stoves, &c.
Maxfield, R. A. — Manufacturer
Nichols, A. F. — Foundry
Nichols, Edwin — Commission Merchant
Norris, Geo. W. — Stable Keeper
Nesmith, Thos. — Real Estate

Noyes, E. J. — Corporation Detective
O'Hearn, P. — Contractor
O'Sullivan, James — Boots, Shoes, &c.
Pollard, A. G. — Dry Goods
Pratt, Amasa — Planing, &c.
Potter, W. E. — Real Estate
Puffer, Jas. F., Jr. — Furniture
Peabody, J. G. — Doors, Sashes, &c.
Pindar, J. H. — Merchant Tailor
Puffer, F. W. — Crockery, &c.
Preston, Jas. F. — Talbot Dyewood Co.
Perham, H. C. — Treasurer K. Mach. Co.
Perkins, M. G. — Real Estate
Palmer, Charles D. —
Pevey, James A. — Iron Foundry
Pike, S. P. — Provisions
Parker, Samuel G. — Man'f'r Soda Water, &c.
Puffer, S. B. — Real Estate
Perkins, F. S. — Machinery Manufacturer
Parker, Percy — Paper Manufacturer
Pickering, J. W. C. — Treas. P. Knitting Co.
Page, Dudley L. — Caterer
Pinder, Jos. L. — Notions, etc.
Putnam, Addison — Clothing
Pickman, John J. — Lawyer
Pindar, Albert — Superintendent
Putnam, F. E. — Restaurant
Prescott, D. M. — Plasterer
Parker, Fred H. — Grocer
Pevey, F. S. — Iron Foundry
Pierce, C. W. — Agent Express Co.
Pearson, James F. — Wholesale Fruit, &c.
Putnam, George E. — Produce Merchant
Partridge, A. V. — Hotel Keeper
Quinn, E. B. — Lawyer
Qua, F. W. — Lawyer
Rice, H. R. — Printer
Rice, Frank E. — M'f'r Wire Goods
Randlett, O. B. — Grocer
Runels, George — Real Estate
Rowell, E. T. — Pres. R. R. Bank.
Russell, A. L. — Real Estate
Reed, William — Stone Contractor
Rogers, George G. — Jeweller
Ripley, R. S. — Iron Foundry
Reed, George G. — Grocer
Shepard, Jesse H. — Real Estate
Stanley, George E. — Coal, Wood, &c.
Spalding, W. H. — Paper Hangings
Shedd, F. B. — Cologne Manufacturer
Stiles, Perry P. — Grocer
Stott, Thomas — Card Clothing
Smith, Caleb L. — Grocer
Stickney, F. W. — Architect
Smith, E. A. — Real Estate
Simpson, O. A. — Contractor
Smith, Melvin B. — Civil Engineer
Stott, Charles A. — Manufacturer
Shaw, Frank E. — Hotel Keeper
Smith, L. J. — Clothing
Stone, Z. E. — Printer
Swett, J. H. — Carriage Manufacturer
Sheppard, J. H. — Florist
Shaw, J. W. B. — Real Estate
Swan, D. A. — Boots, Shoes, &c.
Stevens, Geo. H. — Lawyer
Smith, James T. — Lawyer
Stowell, F. E. — Stable Keeper
Spalding, W. B. — Real Estate
Simpson, R. — Wholesale Grocer
Stiles, J. A. — Grocer

| | | | |
|---|---|---|---|
| Shattuck. E. H. | Hardware | Ward, William H. | Contractor |
| Staples, Arthur | Mason | Wilder, H. H. | Stoves, &c. |
| Stevens, J. Tyler | Real Estate | Wheeler, A. H. | Grocer |
| Stevens, R. L. | Real Estate | Wallace, D. R. | Insurance |
| Saunders, C. W. | Lumber | Wilson Joseph M. | WholesaleD's'd Beef,&c. |
| Sherman, Edward S. | Flour, Grain, &c. | Whithed, Darius | Soap Manufacturer |
| Sherman, Frederick W. | Insurance | White, E. L. | Leather Manufacturer |
| Tucke, E. M. | Insurance | Wiggin, W. H. | Contractor |
| Thompson, H. M. | Felting Manufacturer | White, W. H. | Leather Manufacturer |
| Tweed, T. G. | Apothecary | Wood, Robert | Veterinary Surgeon |
| Tyler, A. S. | Treasurer Sav. Bank | Whittier, N. | Manufacturer Twine |
| Tibbets, H. L. | Lumber | Woodward, G. T. | Carpenter |
| Thompson, Joseph P. | Register of Deeds | Woodworth, A. B. | Lumber, &c. |
| Thompson, A. G. | Real Estate | Wilson, E. A. | Coal, Wood, &c. |
| Taylor, Frederick | Hardware | White, Fred O. | Contractor |
| Trull, Larkin T. | Lawyer | Watson, W. S. | Cop Tube Manufacturer |
| Trull, Jesse N. | Farmer | Welch, John | Furniture Manufacturer |
| Taylor, A. C. | Dry Goods | Wood, George H. | Jeweller |
| Tryder, George H. | Stable Keeper | Wyman, S. B. | Lawyer |
| Thomas, E. W. | Agent T. & S. Mills | Whiting, F. A. | Mortgages, &c. |
| Viles, Jesse A. | Veterinary Surgeon | Ward, George M. | Paper Hangings |
| Varnum, D. H. | Real Estate | Wheelock, A. C. | Real Estate |
| Varnum, L. R. J. | Real Estate | Woodward, John C. | Real Estate |
| Wood, Edward N. | Flour, Grain, &c. | Wing, W. O. | Milk Dealer |
| Wilder, Charles W. | Wholesale Provisions | Young, Samuel | Electrician |

## MASTER BUILDERS' EXCHANGE.

AN ASSOCIATION FOR THE INTERCHANGE OF SOCIAL, ARCHITECTURAL AND BUSINESS
INFORMATION.

The Master Builders' Exchange of Lowell was organized in 1888 and at the present time has a membership of seventy-five. The purpose is to maintain reading and exchange rooms for the master mechanics in the various branches of

61

constructive work employed in the erection of buildings, and to afford facilities for information, and the interchange and discussion of social, architectural and business matters.

The special aims are the defence and security of the best interests of mechanics in the building trades, by providing means and authority whereby members of the exchange may demand and secure honorable dealing among themselves and in their relations to others and the attainment of uniformity of action. The membership is limited to one hundred, and to become a member an individual must be engaged in one of the following trades, viz.:—carpenter, mason, iron worker, granite worker, freestone worker, plasterer, roofer, copper and galvanized iron worker, plumber, painter. The regular meetings of the exchange are held quarterly in the rooms at the corner of Central and Appleton streets, but the directors meet once a month. Upon the request of two members the president will appoint an arbitration committee, and in this way many business troubles are settled every year which otherwise might cause dissatisfaction and annoyance to employes. During the past year the business done by members of the exchange amounted to $3,679,564, and $948,694 was paid for labor. The officers of the exchange: President, C. P. Conant; vice-president, E. S. Foss; secretary, J. H. Coggeshall; treasurer, G. H. Watson; directors, C. P. Conant, Geo. H. Watson, Ether S. Foss, G. W. Bagley, S. D. Butterworth, L. F. Kittredge, J. H. Coggeshall, Wm. E. Bissell, P. Conlon.

MEMBERSHIP LIST.

Following are the members of the exchange: J. W. Bennett, G. A. Bennett, W. H. Wiggin, J. H. Coggeshall, W. E. Farrell, P. F. Conaton, W. G. Howe, A. Bibeault, L. F. Kittredge, Wm. Reed, W. H. Kimball, P. B. Quinn, G. W. Bagley, G. E. Barclay, H. H. Wilder, W. F. Wilder, C. H. Nelson, P. O'Hearn, E. S. Foss, C. H. Burtt, Wilder Bennett, Patrick Corcoran, B. H. Staples, W. H. Staples, Robert Goulding, W. C. Gould, John Sweatt, Jonathan Rollins, B. F. Sargent, W. A. Mack, G. H. Watson, Chas. Runels, F. O. White, G. H. Kirby, H. E. Fletcher, W. E. Livingston, W. H. Hope, Joel Knapp, A. P. Knapp, W. H. Spalding, A. W. Harris, G. M. Ward, T. Costello, J. Costello, D. Cushing, J. L. Cushing, W. E Bissell, R. H. Wilson, F. H. Connell, S. D. Butterworth, H. W. Ladd, C. P. Conant, W. H. Fuller, Jr., Patrick Conlon, J. A. Bartlett, F. B. Dow, F. C. Beharrell, James Whittet, Colin McDonald, H. Sutherland, F. B. Taylor, C. F. Varnum, J. B. Varnum, S. H. Jones, P. David, Jr., D. M. Prescott, J. C. Cheney, Jr, Edward Cawley, L. D.Gumb, J. F. Murphy, F. A. Sturtevant, E. E. Galer, B. Scannell, D. Wholey, C. B. Coburn, C. H. Coburn, F. F. Coburn, Mark Holmes, C.W.Holmes,S.H.Geddes, Wm. Kelley, A. L. Brooks, E. N. Morrill, F. E. Lewis, A. K. Pierce, F. W. Howe, J. F. Howe, H. C. Howe, Crawford Burnham, C. O. Davis, Amasa Pratt & Co., Samuel Young & Co., electricians.

# LIBRARIES.

## LIBRARIES WHICH ARE MAINTAINED BY PRIVATE SUBSCRIPTION.

In addition to the City Library which has been described elsewhere, Lowell is well provided with other libraries of a semi-private nature.

Chief among them is the library of the Middlesex Mechanics association. The founding of this society is an excellent sample of the spirit of self-help, and social and educational advancement which has always been manifest among the masses of Lowell's population. The association was founded as an association of mechanics only in 1825. It erected a building of its own in 1835 at a cost of $20,000. The collection of the library proper was begun in 1827, and the library was opened in its present quarters, with the completion of the new building, in 1835.

The library embraces upwards of 22,000 carefully selected volumes, maintains a reading room, and is increased annually from an appropriation of about $500. The association owns a considerable collection of portraits of persons who have been at one time or other identified with Lowell and its growth. The association gives lectures or concerts, or both, during the winter season from the proceeds of which, and from private contributions, it derives its support.

This library is under the supervision of Miss Abby Sargent, and its privileges are enjoyed by a large number of subscribers. The annual fee is a nominal one of $5.

The library of the Middlesex North Agricultural society, consisting of about 400 volumes treating mainly of agricultural subjects, has in recent years been made a part of the Mechanics library.

The library of the Young Men's Catholic association contains in the neighborhood of 1200 volumes, selected mainly with reference to the needs and tastes of the members of the association.

The Mathew and Burke Temperance Institutes, each maintain a library for the use of their members. These collections are made up from standard works of fiction ; history, biography, general literature

also form a part. In connection with these libraries are maintained reading rooms in which are to be found a liberal selection from the magazine and periodical literature of the day.

The Young Men's Christian association possesses about 1000 volumes, together with standard books of reference and a reading room. This library is one that is fast increasing not only in the number of its volumes but in its general usefulness as well.

The People's club maintains a library of some 1600 volumes, which are divided for use between the men's and women's branches of that club. The club supports two reading rooms, and its library is much used.

The library of the Old Resident's Historical association is fast becoming an invaluable collection of information concerning matters pertaining to Lowell and its early history. This library now numbers something like 500 volumes, including a collection of papers read at the quarterly meetings of the association.

NEW MOODY SCHOOL.

## NEWSPAPERS.

### LOWELL HAS SEVEN DAILY DISPENSERS OF INFORMATION.

Lowell is more abundantly supplied with newspapers than any city of its approximate size in New England. The large number of daily newspapers has brought about a sharp competition that has made itself felt in a natural raising of the standard of the news service, with a corresponding depression in advertising rates.

In addition to the city circulation, the newspapers of Lowell as a rule reach a considerable number of readers in the surrounding towns whose inhabitants purchase their supplies in Lowell.

Lowell has two morning and five evening newspapers. The morning newspapers are the Lowell Morning Mail, republican, and the Lowell Morning Times, democratic.

The evening newspapers are the Lowell Daily Citizen, republican; the Lowell Daily Courier, republican; the Lowell Daily News, democratic; the Lowell Evening Mail, issued from the office of the Morning Mail, and the Evening Star, issued from the office of the Morning Times. The Daily News and the Evening Star are one cent newspapers: all others thus far enumerated are two cents.

The Saturday Evening Mail is issued in connection with the morning and evening editions of the same paper.

The American Citizen is issued on Thursday by the Citizen Newspaper company.

The Lowell Journal (weekly) is issued by Marden & Rowell, also proprietors of the Lowell Daily Courier.

The Vox Populi is issued on Wednesdays and Saturdays and is republican in politics.

The Lowell Sun is issued on Saturdays and is democratic in politics.

The Sunday Critic is issued on Sunday mornings and is democratic.

The Sunday Arena is issued on Sunday mornings and is republican in politics.

Three newspapers in the French language are issued in Lowell, L'Etoile, semi-weekly, republican; Le National, daily, democratic; and Le Drapeau National, weekly.

There are a number of other publications issued in Lowell, including a publication by the students of the Lowell high school, a monthly magazine, and several others of a semi-advertising nature.

## HOSPITALS.

### WHERE THE SICK AND THE MAIMED MAY FIND RESCUE.

Lowell has two well equipped hospitals, the usefulness of which has become more apparent as the population increases. The first of these, known as the Lowell, or Corporation Hospital, was established in 1839 for the use of persons employed by the various corporations of the city. The location of this hospital is one of the finest for its purpose in the city, being upon high ground overlooking the Merrimack river. The management of this hospital is vested in a board of trustees composed of the local agents of the various corporations together with two other citizens, one of whom shall be the mayor of the city. Since 1881 the hospital has been in charge of a staff of visiting physicians and surgeons who give their services gratuitously.

The hospital buildings are commodious

and well arranged and furnish ample accommodation for about fifty patients at a time. The hospital treats on an average three hundred patients a year, exclusive of its out-patient department, established in 1877, which is conducted under its separate staff and which is made accessible not only to the employes of the corporations, but to the general poor of the city.

St. John's Hospital is an efficient institution, established in 1866 by Sister Emerentiana at the suggestion of the bishop of the diocese, and operated under the supervision of the order of the Sisters of Charity. From small beginnings, this hospital has grown in size, as it has been obliged to meet the increasing demands upon its services.

The hospital accommodates about one hundred house patients, and treats from

MARSTON BUILDING, MIDDLESEX STREET.

four to five hundred patients a year. Three times that number are treated in its out-patient department, which is conducted, as in the case of the Lowell Hospital, under a staff especially appointed for that work.

The hospital is to-day supported by the contributions of the public. It knows no creed nor color; nor are its doors ever closed upon the poor. Of the whole number of patients treated since it was established, nearly two-thirds have been charity patients. It is to all intents and purposes a city hospital, and all cases of accident, other than those which occur in the mills, are taken there for treatment. The staff includes the foremost physicians and surgeons in the city, who give their services gratuitously. The institution is of brick, located in Belvidere, and finely equipped.

In connection with the hospital two free dispensaries are maintained. The Lowell Dispensary was incorporated in 1836, and is maintained by a fund derived from private contributions and from membership fees. The annual income of this fund is devoted to the purchase of medicines for the relief of the worthy sick poor.

The City Dispensary, established by ordinance in 1879, is supported by an annual appropriation of $1000 for the distribution of medicines to the sick poor. Twelve physicians are chosen to serve for one year. In 1889, 1837 prescriptions were compounded. The institution is conducted under the supervision of the overseers of the poor.

This department also maintains an efficient ambulance service, with its physician especially appointed. The value of this service has proven itself so great that the city will undoubtedly increase its facilities by the addition of a second ambulance within a short time.

## THE CHURCHES.

### FORTY-FOUR TEMPLES DEVOTED TO THE WORSHIP OF GOD.

There are forty-four churches in Lowell. Some of them are handsome, pretentious buildings, others are modestly suited to the spirit of their congregations. Of the forty-four, thirty-six belong to Protestant denominations, seven to the Catholic faith, and one to Judaism. There are besides these, several missions and the Young Men's Christian Association.

Pawtucket—This Congregational church was incorporated June 22, 1797. It is the oldest church in the city. Its present pastor is the Rev. Charles H. Willcox.

First Congregational.—This society was organized June 6, 1826. The church is a handsome brick edifice, costing $60,000. It is located on Merrimack street, directly opposite the new Memorial building. It has now no settled pastor.

The Eliot.—This Congregational church was organized in 1830, and was named in honor of the famous apostle to the Indians. The church is an imposing brick edifice, situated on Summer street and overlooking the South Common. The pastor is the Rev. Dr. J. M. Greene, who has been its minister since 1870.

John Street.—This Congregational society was organized in 1839. The present church edifice was built in 1840. The present pastor is the Rev. Henry T. Rose, who was installed in 1883.

Kirk Street.—This is another Congregational church. It was organized in 1845. The present church was built in 1846 at a cost of $23,000. It has several times been renovated and altered. The present pastor is the Rev. Dr. Malcolm McGregor Dana, who was installed Oct. 11, 1888.

High Street.—Another Congregational church, established in 1846. The edifice stands on a commanding elevation. It is of wood with a battlemented tower, which is a landmark in the community. Plans have been prepared for a new and more substantial structure. The present pastor is the Rev. Charles W. Huntington, who was installed in 1888.

Highland Congregational.—A handsome structure of brick, located on Westford street, and completed in 1884. There is no settled pastor at this time.

French Protestant.—A Congregational church, with edifice of stone, on Bowers street. The present pastor is the Rev. Joseph H. Paradis.

St. Anne's.—When Lowell was a town and the Merrimack company the controlling industrial and social factor of the community of 1200 souls, St. Anne's was established. Kirk Boott was a Episcopalian and he established an Episcopal church in 1824. Previous to that time religious services had been held in a two story wooden building on Merrimack street. In that year the Rev. Theodore Edson was called to be the minister of the church and on March 16, 1825, the present picturesque stone edifice was erected. Dr. Edson remained its rector until his death in June, 1883, after a faithful service of 59 years. His ministry was a remarkable one and he died in the full odor of sanctity —a man beloved and venerated by all the people. The present rector is the Rev. Dr. A. St. John Chambre. Attached to the church is the Edson orphanage for boys.

In the tower of the church is a chime of bells famous throughout New England for their sweet toned melody.

St. John's.—This is a picturesque Episcopal church edifice on Gorham street. The society was organized in 1860. The Rev. Leander C. Manchester has been rector since 1873.

House of Prayer.—A small wooden church on Walker street devoted to worship of the ritualistic order. The present rector is the Rev. J. Q. Davis.

First Presbyterian.—It was organized in 1869, and worships in an old but very substantial building on Appleton street. Rev. Robert Court, D. D., is the learned pastor.

Westminster Presbyterian.—It is soon to enter a pleasant wooden church on Tyler street. The society is three years old and Rev. J. O. Campbell is the pastor.

First Baptist.—The edifice on Church street was built soon after the society was organized in 1826, but it has since been modernized. Rev. Alexander Blackburn is the pastor.

Worthen Street Baptist.—This is one of the most picturesque churches in the city. It is of brick and of the Italian style of architecture. The society was organized in 1831, and W. S. Ayres is the pastor.

Branch Street Tabernacle. — A large wooden building with a seating capacity of 1500. The society is Baptist and was organized in 1869. The pastor is Rev. O. E. Mallory.

Fifth Street Baptist.—A pleasant wooden chapel belonging to a society that was organized in 1874. Rev. L. G. Barrett has looked out for the spiritual wants of the church since Jan. 1, 1888.

Paige Street Baptist.—This society, organized in 1833, is of the Free Will order. The church is of brick, severely plain in design without, but inviting within. Rev. George N. Howard was installed as its pastor in 1885.

Mt. Vernon Church.—A pleasant chapel in a somewhat elevated location. The society was organized as F. W. Baptist in 1874, and Rev. C. S. Frost is acting pastor.

Chelmford Street Church. — A cosy brick building, built soon after the organization of the F. W. Baptist society in 1880. Rev. H. Lockhart is pastor.

St. Paul's Church.—Situated between Warren and Hurd streets. It is high, of the style of twenty years ago. The interior is lit by electricity. The society, which is sixty-four years old, was the first of the Methodist Episcopal denomination organized in the city. Rev. W. H. Thomas was appointed its pastor in April of the current year.

Worthen Street Methodist.—Organized in 1838. It occupies a renovated wooden church opposite that of the Baptists. Rev. G. C. Osgood is the pastor.

Central Methodist.—It is situated at the corner of John and Paige streets, and is similar in design to the Baptist church in its rear. Rev. J. N. Short is entering upon the fourth year of his pastorate. The society was organized in 1843.

Highland Methodist.—It is pleasantly located on Loring street. The society was organized in 1875, and the present pastor, Rev. Alexander Dight, secured his appointment in 1889.

Centralville Methodist.—This substantial brick church at the corner of Bridge and Hildreth streets, has not yet been occupied a month. Rev. Sullivan Holman, who organized the society in 1887, has been a preacher for more than fifty years.

First Primitive Methodist. — A wooden church on Gorham street. The society has been in existence for more than twenty years, and Rev. T. M. Bateman is its pastor.

Berean Primitive Methodist.—A wooden chapel on Moore street. The society was the outgrowth of a mission established in 1884. Rev. T. G. Spencer has been its pastor for three years.

Unitarian Church. — In the upper story of a building on Merrimack street. The society, organized in 1829, supports a number of excellent social and literary fraternities. Rev. George Batchelor is the pastor.

Ministry-at-Large.—Situated on Middlesex street, and organized in 1843 under the auspices of the Unitarian society. Its aim is to befriend the worthy poor. Rev. G. C. Wright is in charge.

First Universalist.-A noble brick church on Hurd street built at a cost of $80,000. Its interior is one of the finest in the city. The society was organized in 1827 and the pastor, Rev. George W. Bicknell, was installed in December. 1879.

Second Universalist.—A sombre stone church on Shattuck street. Rev. R. A. Green has been the pastor for eighteen years. The society dates from 1836.

Advent Christian Church.—Organized in 1846 and worshiping in a church on Grand street. Elder J. Ward is the preacher.

Swedish Evangelican Church.—Situated on Meadowcroft street within easy reach of many Swedish families. Rev. J. V. Soderman is the pastor. The society was organized in 1882.

Swedish Evangelical Mission.--It is of the Congregational faith and was organized six years ago. It is situated on London street with Rev. Emil Holmblad as its pastor.

St. Patrick's Church.—A substantial stone edifice on Fenwick street. In its lofty tower is a set of melodious chimes. The society was organized in 1827 as the first of the Catholic faith. The rector is Rev. Michael O'Brien and his assistants are Rev. J. A. Gleason, Rev. J. J. Shaw and Rev. Thomas Burke.

St. Peter's Church.— At present a temporary structure on Gorham street awaiting the building of a costly church opposite the court house. Its rectors are Rev. Michael Ronan, Rev. James McKenna and Rev. Thomas D. McManus. The society was established in 1841.

St. Joseph's Church.--A substantial granite building on Lee street. The society is twenty-three years old and is in charge of Revs. A. M. Garin, Alexander Founier, C. Lagier, A. Gladu and A. Marion.

Immaculate Conception.—A magnificent granite church of the Gothic order. It is the largest in the city and has a seating capacity of 2,000. Rev. W. D. Joyce is the rector and he has several assistants. The society was established in 1869.

St. Michael's Church.—Another Catholic society organized in 1883. Only the lower portion of its brick church on Sixth street is finished. Rev. William O'Brien and Rev. J. Gilday are the rectors.

The Sacred Heart.—A church on Moore street which is also unfinished. The organization of the society took place in 1884 and the present rectors are Rev. J. M. Guillard and Rev. D. M. Burns.

St. Jean Baptiste.—This society was organized in 1889 and worships in the basement of what in time will be a fine brick church on Merrimack street. Rev. J. W. Pelletier is in charge and he is assisted by Revs. J. T. Lavoie, A. A. Amyot and R. Marion.

## THE CITY OF THE DEAD.

The "resting places" of Lowell's dead, consecrated spots in our very midst, ever reminding us of the uncertainty of our earthly existence, are six in number, four of them being located on the southerly outskirts of the city. There have been other cemeteries within the boundaries in the early days of the city, whose small area becoming encroached upon by the growth of the city have finally been taken up as residential sites after the cemetery itself had been condemned. Of these the incomplete state of the city's records in the early days has prevented the gathering of statistics relative to the opening of, the area and number of graves in each,

making a history of Lowell's cemeteries quite incomplete. Of the early cemeteries, that condemned in 1846, located in East Merrimack, just above the junction of Nesmith and Alder streets, was probably the oldest, and in it undoubtedly were interred the bodies of the pioneers who cleared the land on what is now the city.

This cemetery was condemned by the city council in 1846 and the last body removed to the Lowell cemetery in the summer of 1847. Another cemetery, of small area, of whose early history there is no record, is the School street burying ground, containing less than half an acre, which half a century ago was used by a few prominent and wealthy families as a private cemetery. With the inception of other places, however, many lots passed into other hands until no more graves could be opened. With the exception of interments in family lots of members of the family originally owning the lots there have been no interments for nearly a decade. At periods a movement arises to have the cemetery condemned, on the sanitary grounds, but the opposition likely to arise from lot owners precludes vigorous forwarding of that plan.

The oldest cemetery, of which the opening date is known, is what is now called No. 2 yard, or the old Lowell burying ground, the first grave in which was opened on August 15, 1835. It is located on Gorham street directly opposite the Fair grounds and is of limited area, barely exceeding an acre. There have been but few interments, and those only in family lots, the past decade. For a long period the place was neglected but now its appearance is that of a well kept and carefully looked after garden.

Adjoining it on the south is the Catholic cemetery, of large area, and beyond it the Edson cemetery, owned by the city, comprising about fourteen acres of land extending to the Chelmsford line. This cemetery was opened in September, 1846, after the city had authorized the purchase of a small tract of land. The first interment was in the following December. The management until this year was entirely in the hands of the mayor, who appointed the superintendent and looked after the city's interests. This being the only municipal burying ground frequent additions of land have been necessary, and at the present time there is no available space for new graves. The purchase of additional land has therefore become necessary and the appointment of a board of trustees to assume management will probably result in the purchase of additional territory. The trustees, appointed under a special enactment of the general court, are Fred E. Woodies and Frank B. Dow, confirmed by the board of aldermen June 30th. The Edson cemetery is a beautiful place and though the city has not lavished a very large sum upon it, there is a stone chapel of quaint architecture just inside the main entrance. The land is quite level and the careful way in which the paths and avenues have been laid out makes the place pleasing to the eye.

The largest cemetery is the Lowell, with its 84 acres of land, at the foot of the southerly slope of Fort Hill park, the main entrance into which is from Lawrence street, nearly opposite the railway station of the Boston & Maine railroad. In the cemetery are the evidences of the expenditure of a vast amount of wealth. There are magnificent monuments and memorials almost without number, and the natural beauties of the place have been greatly enhanced by the skill of the architect, the engineer and the gardener. The cemetery is owned by a corporation, chartered in 1841, and the management is vested in a board of trustees.

There are about 13,000 graves in the cemetery, and the demand for lots is always vigorous. Last year, by an act of legislature, the corporation was allowed to buy, sell and hold real estate, and accordingly 9½ acres of land were purchased. The new purchase is now being laid out, and it is to have an entrance from Rogers street in Belvidere. The Lawrence street entrance is through a magnificent granite gate, surmounted by a bell presented the corporation in 1886 by Mrs. Hocum Hosford, as a memorial to her husband, the late ex-Mayor Hocum Hosford. There is also the chapel, a structure which in itself adds much to the beauty of the grounds. Among the memorials are many imported statues and designs in carved marble. Among the most notable will be the colossal marble lion, designed and sculptured by Mr. Joy in his London studio, and which is to be placed in the family lot of J. C. Ayer.

The officers of the corporation are Charles L. Knapp, president; John H. McAlvin treasurer; L. R. J. Varnum, A. A. Coburn, D. M. Prescott, C. D. Starbird, Francis Jewett, August Fels, A. A. Blanchard, C. A. Stott, W. H. Wiggin, H. H. Wilder, G. L. Hildreth and Z. E. Stone, trustees; Robert H. Mulno, superintendent.

The last cemetery to be mentioned is called by the family name of those who are the principal lot holders — The Hildreth Burying Ground. It is the smallest of the cemeteries and is on Hildreth street in Centralville. Here are interred the remains of members of the Hildreth family, and of a few of the earliest residents of that section before it became a part of the city. Here also is the family lot of a distinguished townsman, Gen. Benjamin F.

Butler. There are no evidences of wealth in the appearance of its gravestones; it is the facsimile of a country burial place in the midst of a district which is rapidly being built over by houses of the working people.

Such are the cemeteries of the city—the places set apart for the distinct and particular purpose of burying the dead, the places he'd sacred—where the living may visit to hold communion in sweet memories and visions of the past.

## PLEASURE RESORTS.

### THE OPPORTUNITIES FOR RECREATION IN AND ABOUT LOWELL.

Lowell is peculiarly favored in the advantages it enjoys for recreation and natural pleasure. It is built on both sides of the picturesque Merrimack where it rushes through the gorge of mica schist and gneiss. Its banks are high and clothed with trees, and here as at Indian Orchard are most delightful bits of sequestered shade.

The Concord river, so placid and so classical, also flows through Lowell, and is no less picturesque in its way than the Merrimack, with which it is wedded. These two rivers afford a never ending and never wearying source of healthful pleasure. The Merrimack flows through a piney region, and there are no less than six steamers which are licensed to carry passengers. Some of these run to Nashua, 14 miles up the river; but canoeists can go a dozen miles farther without meeting an obstruction. Others of the steamers ply between the city and Tyng's Island, a popular pleasure resort, Harmony Grove in Tyngsboro and Woodlawn, all summer resorts.

The Vesper Boat Club with 150 members, is established in an elegant club house on Pawtucket street. It controls a numerous navy of canoes and row boats, and counts among its members some of the crack sailing canoeists of the country. There is no other boat club on the Merrimack, but there are several boat houses.

On the Concord there is an unbroken stretch of four miles to North Billerica. There the carry is over the bank into the old canal, and then there is an unobstructed passage to Old Concord and Saxonville beyond. Many canoeists make the trip of the Concord. Starting at Sudbury and entering the Merrimack at Lowell they go down to Newburyport and the sea.

There are two clubs of limited membership on the Concord, the Wamesit and the Musquetaquid.

Mascuppic Lake, otherwise known as Tyng's Pond, is situated at the foot of Whortleberry hill, four miles from Lowell. It is reached by the electric line of the Lowell & Suburban Street Railway Company. The company owns two sides of the lake. At one end is the Lakeview pavilion where excellent food is served. Here, too, are the bowling alleys and the dance hall. On the southerly shore are Mountain Rock and Mascuppic groves. The former is fitted with pavilion, dance hall and bowling alley for private picnic parties; the latter is reserved for camping purposes. The pines surrounding the lake are particularly tall and the spot is one of the loveliest conceivable. Willow Dale, on the eastern shore of the lake, is an old established and popular resort kept by Jona. Bowers.

This lake affords the people of Lowell cheap and perfect pleasure. The round trip costs 25 cents, and it ensures a ride of ten miles in the electric cars through a beautiful country, a ride around the lake on the steamer Mascuppic and free dancing every afternoon and evening. The last car leaves Lakeview at 10.15, and there are no intoxicating liquors permitted on the place.

Haggett's pond in Andover is five miles from Lowell. It is exceedingly popular with small parties.

Nabnassett pond in Chelmsford, four miles away, is a beautiful sheet of water, and is quite popular with picnic parties. Other picnic resorts within easy distance of Lowell are Baptist pond, Long pond, Canobie lake, Silver lake and Shawsheen grove. Robin's hill in Chelmsford affords a fine view of the surrounding country.

But Lowell is within an hour's ride of the sea shore and Boston is only 45 minutes away. Lake Winnepesaukee can be reached in two hours and one may dine in Lowell and eat supper at the Fabyan house the same night.

But while Nature is generous, Art is not unmindful. Fort Hill Park is unique, and unlike any other park in New England. The hill has an elevation of 200 feet above the level of the rivers and the prospect is a fine one. The park was the gift of Miss Elizabeth Rogers and was put in its present attractive condition by Messrs. Shedd, Smith and Garity free of expense to the city. The North and South commons are quite roomy breathing places, and Park Garden beautifies Belvidere.

The Lowell Opera House is without a peer. It was built in 1889 by Fay Bros.

& Hosford at a cost of $100,000. It seats 1500 people and is a model of beauty. Its conveniences are such as modern comfort demands. It is lighted throughout with electricity, and the stage appointments will compare very favorably with those of any metropolitan theatre. The lessee and manager is Mr. John F. Cosgrove.

Music Hall is a cosy and comfortable little theatre, where plays are performed at popular prices. The present lessees are Litchfield, Watson & Thomas. They give nightly performances and employ a stock company.

## BUILDING OPERATIONS.

### THREE MILLIONS OF MONEY BEING USED IN ERECTING SUBSTANTIAL STRUCTURES.

Competent authorities place the value of the stone and brick buildings now in process of construction in Lowell at $2,000,000, and the value of the wooden buildings at $1,000,000.

Among the principal buildings are the new City hall, the Memorial building, the Odd Fellows' block, a block at the corner of Bridge and East Merrimack streets, one on the opposite corner on Prescott street, F. G. Mitchell's block on Merrimack street, the Edson block on Merrimack street, buildings for the Kittredge heirs and A. G. Pollard on Middle street, and the U. S. Government building and a High School, the sites of which are already being cleared.

It will be seen that work is assured for many months to hundreds of laborers employed in the construction of such buildings.

## AVAILABLE LAND.

The following is a description of the land available for manufacturing purposes within the city and in the suburban villages. The letters refer to the locations given in the map.

The map, to which especial attention is directed, was prepared from the latest maps by the state survey. It shows an area a little short of that included in the city of Worcester, and evidences the opportunities there are for development in this city and neighborhood. The plan of Lowell, which occupies the centre of the map, shows the street railway lines, the steam railway lines and the waterways.

On itare displayed letters which on referring to the following list will be found to locate territory that is advisable for manufacturing purposes.

---

#### BELVIDERE.

Belvidere, with the exception of the land bordering on the railway, is a residential section of the most desirable character. The land excepted is admirably adapted for manufacturing purposes. The Electric Light company has placed its elaborate station there and the White Brothers & Sons have recently erected a three story brick factory in that neighborhood. The land is traversed by the Lowell and Andover railroad which has close connection with the Framingham branch of the Old Colony.

(A) Strip of land having 1000 feet frontage on the railroad, held for manufacturing purposes, Smith and Shedd, trustees. Smith and Shedd are also trustees for a lot of land on Boylston street (B) having 800 feet frontage on the railroad. On the opposite side of Boylston street is the Oakland territory. There is also considerable territory (c) abutting on the railroad in this section which is the property of W. H. Wiggin and Miss Elizabeth Rogers. There is water in sufficient supply from springs and brooks, and the railroad facilities are unexcelled. There is a great area of adjoining land which, at a reasonable outlay, can be used for residences.

## OAKLANDS.

Taking Rogers street as the dividing line, Oaklands extends in a more level expansion eastward to beyond the tracks of the Boston & Lowell Railroad. Here (D D) is an immense tract of land, a loamy soil resting upon a hard clay foundation. It is flanked on the south by Boylston street, and extends for half a mile toward Phenix on both sides of the railroad. There is no more available land in the city of Lowell for manufacturing purposes, water is found in ample volume at a depth of a few feet, and the railroad affords facilities for transportation of an exceptional character. It is the purpose of Messrs. Shepard, Russell and Fuller to have a spur track running through the land lying between Hanover Avenue and the Phenix line.

The most of this land is within the town of Tewksbury where the taxes are only $11.50 per m; and with good roads, ample water supply and railroad facilities, there is no reason why manufacturers should not find this a place of exceptional advantages. Gas from the Lowell company is an additional privilege. This land upon which manufactories may be established lies on both sides of the track and beyond it on the rising ground is territory which can be bought for little money upon which to erect houses for those who may be employed in that vicinity.

The land lies a mile and a half from the Post office and is reached by horse cars and steam railway tracks, there is a station at Phenix where the Atherton Machine Company, is established, and employs 400 men, and the car fares on both train and street railway are five cents.

The syndicate make this generous offer: They will give the land to any manufacturer that may desire to build an establishment in that locality. The quality of help that can be secured is reliable, and the advantage which close connection with the city assures makes the opportunity worth in every way the attention of manufacturers.

There is another thing to be remembered, and that is the fact that this land is less than a mile distant from the Electric Light Station, which is now equipped to furnish from 1 to 100 horse power.

## AYERS CITY.

"Ayers City" is a large section of the city indicated on the maps by the letters E E. It is traversed by River Meadow Brook, a stream of considerable size, which furnishes some 50 horse power, and by the Old Colony railroad, having direct communication with New York. There is also a spur track connecting with the Lowell and Andover branch of the Boston and Maine railroad. This ensures direct communication with Portland and with Boston. The land is of a very desirable character, being level and surrounded by high lands which are in great demand for residential purposes.

Near the Old Colony freight house, which is located at the junction of the Framingham with the Boston and Lowell road, and on the westerly side of the brook, is three acres of land, the property of George W. Chase. There is a street cut through from Chelmsford street to the brook, not indicated on the map, and the land enjoys excellent water privileges. Mr. Chase, who is a master builder, will erect upon this land and lease to responsible parties at moderate terms any kind of factory they may desire. He will also erect houses and tenements for the help, that shall be near at hand. He has a two story factory, new, with elevator and steam heat, which he is prepared to lease on acceptable terms. The street railway line on Chelmsford street is close at hand.

Near this property is land owned by O. O. Greenwood, two acres bordering on the brook.

There are two or three acres belonging to Alanson Folsom.

There are two and one half acres of the Hubbard estate which border on Chelmsford street.

George Parsons owns seven acres which adjoins the brook.

There are three acres of the Kimball estate with excellent railroad facilities.

On the easterly side of the brook there is a spur track running from the Framingham branch to the Arey and Maddock tannery and the Criterion Company's Knitting Mill. There is much valuable land here having brook privileges.

J. B. Francis owns an acre and more between the brook and the track.

E. B. Peirce owns several acres on the railroad. The J. Q. Hubbard heirs own several acres and so, too, do the Conner Brothers whose coal sheds mark the terminus of the spur track.

On the higher land on the easterly side of the Framingham branch, Messrs. J. W. Bennett and Robert Bartlett own four acres having a frontage of 600 feet on the railroad running south from the point where the cross section starts to unite with the Boston and Maine road. It is dry land and admirably located for iron workers.

Beyond the Bennett and Bartlett land lie the acres of Capt. Joseph P. Thompson. They extend southerly to the land of the Parkman heirs (F), which, crossing the city line into Chelmsford, is 300 acres in extent. The Parker heirs also own a level stretch of land to the east of the Bennett and Bartlett land.

On the westerly side of the Framingham track, at its junction with the spur connecting with the Boston and Maine road is the land of the Osgood estate.

George Runels owns a level stretch opposite the Dobbins Boiler Works on the line of the spur track.

Thissell and Lamson, and Charles Cowley also own land in this vicinity having brook and railroad privileges. The growth of this section of the city has been phenomenal and it is rapidly becoming a populous district.

### MIDDLESEX VILLAGE.

This section is admirably adapted for manufacturing purposes. It is traversed by the Lowell and Nashua railroad which has through connections with Canada and the Pacific coast. At the easterly end, near the junction of Middlesex and Pawtucket streets, Black brook, a stream of considerable volume, flows into the Merrimack. Quite a pond is formed here by the back water from the river. This water is available for manufacturing purposes.

A plentiful supply of water may also be secured by digging or boring twenty feet below the surface.

The land is level and there is much of it vacant on both sides of the road and along the line of the railroad all the way to the busy village of North Chelmsford.

Although there used to be glass works and hat shops in Middlesex Village before Lowell was established, there is now only one manufacturing establishment in operation there. The pioneer of the modern industrial movement is the J. W. C. Pickering Company which has just completed a handsome two story brick mill.

Every acre of land lying between the highway and the railroad, and Pickering's mill and the city line (G) is available and desirable for manufacturing purposes. The owners are as follows and their property lies west of Pickering's mill in the sequence given:

H. K. Ferrin, 1 1-2 acres, abutting on railroad.

James T. Smith, 1 1-2 acres, abutting on railroad.

Heirs of Joseph Smith, 3 acres, abutting on railroad.

C. E. Carter, 3 acres, abutting on railroad.

Mrs. Samuel Tyler, 5 acres, abutting on railroad.

Samuel P. Hadley, 2 acres abutting on railroad.

Mrs. Parker, several acres, abutting on railroad.

Frederick F. Ayer, 5 acres, abutting on railroad.

Land abutting on Black brook and lying west of Stevens street toward the city limits (H).

The W. E. Livingston estate is one of the finest in the city. It comprises 40 acres intersected by streets and available for residential or manufacturing purposes. There are 10 acres bordering on the easterly side of Black brook. This land is level, the supply of water is copious and never-failing and of an excellent quality.

Southerly from the Livingston place, and abutting on the brook, lie 3 acres owned by George McIntire, several acres owned by George Holden and 3 acres owned by Wallace McIntire. All these owners have rights in the waters of the brook.

West of the brook, and lying between it and the highway (J) are the following properties:

John B. Richardson land, on which are several ice houses, the brook furnishing a sufficient supply to stock them. This is admirable land for manufacturing purposes.

Stillman B. Clough, 4 acres abutting on the brook.

Mrs. John Webber, 9 acres, abutting on the brook.

Mrs. Wentworth, several acres, abutting on the brook.

Mrs. S. Tyler, several acres, abutting on the brook.

The Marshall Pratt estate, W. E. Potter and Son, agents, a large tract on both sides of the brook.

Joseph Bowers, a large tract on both sides of the brook.

While the land here mentioned is desirable for manufacturers, it is flanked on the south by rising land (K) which is being rapidly utilized for residences. It is cheap and manufacturers can find ready accommodations there for their help.

There is a railroad station at Middlesex Village, and the street railway will be extended through that section this year to the city line. The distance from the city post office is a mile and a half.

## CENTRALVILLE.

In Centralville, north of the Aiken street bridge and lying between Lakeview avenue and Beaver brook (N), is land the property of John Ames, August Fels and David Skillings. This section is particularly recommended for shoe shops.

East of this land and lying between Lakeview avenue and Bridge street, is Crescent Hill (O), a recently opened territory, which is being rapidly utilized for residences. Its streets are graded and lighted, and gas, city water and sewerage are among the privileges the residents enjoy. It is but a few minutes walk from Dracut woolen mills and but a short distance from the great corporations with which it is connected by the Aiken street bridge.

## OTHER LAND.

In addition to the lands in these sections which are desirable for manufacturing purposes, there are twelve acres belonging to the proprietors of the locks and canals at the bend of the river near the Aiken street bridge (L), which can be leased for manufacturing purposes.

They also have two acres of land on Broadway (N) which they will lease at reasonable terms.

In the neighborhood of Gorham street and lying between that thoroughfare and the Concord river is much land desirable for manufacturing purposes. At the junction of the street with the railroad is the land of the Osgood heirs.

There are 3 acres (P) for which W. E. Potter & Son are agents.

(R) The Appleton heirs own six acres.

Mrs. Jeremiah O'Neil owns 15 acres.

James Meadowcroft owns several acres.

Timothy Doolan owns 3 acres and will welcome a factory on his land. All this land has water privileges in the Concord river and lies between the tracks of the Boston & Lowell and the Lowell & Salem railroads.

The Nesmith heirs own a fine lot for manufacturing purposes (S) on Willie street.

## IN THE SUBURBS.

### DRACUT.

There is a vast extent of available territory in this town, abutting on the Electric railway and on Beaver Brook.

The brook furnishes 125 horse power for the Collins mills in Collinsville, for the Parker and Bassett paper mills and for the Merrimack woolen mills. The village is within ten minutes ride of the city post office.

The following is the available land:

(T) Sixty-four acres owned by Percy Parker. This land abuts on the brook and is admirably adapted for manufacturers. With it go the privileges of the brook, and power may be obtained by the erection of a plant on the westerly side of the dam.

The Goodhue land lies south of the Parker land and between the highway and the brook (U).

The land lying west and north of the Parker land is owned by O. J. Coburn, and is traversed by the brook. There is a fall here which is not utilized.

Richard Bennett also owns a lot with water privileges.

### NORTH CHELMSFORD.

North Chelmsford possesses many valuable advantages for manufacturers. It is traversed by the Lowell & Nashua and Stony brook railroads. It lies on the westerly bank of the Merrimack, into which flow two brooks of considerable volume, the Stony brook and Deep brook. Here is the available land:

www.ingramcontent.com/pod-product-compliance
Lightning Source LLC
Chambersburg PA
CBHW030017030726
47499CB00008B/3036